THE RIVER BELOW

THE RIVER BELOW

Bonnie Hearn Hill

This first world edition published 2017
in Great Britain and the USA by
SEVERN HOUSE PUBLISHERS LTD of
19 Cedar Road, Sutton, Surrey, England, SM2 5DA.
Trade paperback edition first published
in Great Britain and the USA 2018 by
SEVERN HOUSE PUBLISHERS LTD.

British Library Cataloguing in Publication Data
A CIP catalogue record for this title is available from the British Library.

ISBN-13: 978-0-7278-8745-0 (cased)
ISBN-13: 978-1-84751-859-0 (trade paper)
ISBN-13: 978-1-78010-921-3 (e-book)

All Severn House titles are printed on acid-free paper.

Severn House Publishers support the Forest Stewardship Council™ [FSC™],
the leading international forest certification organisation.
All our titles that are printed on FSC certified paper carry the FSC logo.

Typeset by Palimpsest Book Production Ltd.,
Falkirk, Stirlingshire, Scotland.
Printed and bound in Great Britain by
TJ International, Padstow, Cornwall.

For Hazel Dixon-Cooper and Wendy Cooper,
and to the river

ACKNOWLEDGMENTS

After sixteen years, Laura Dail is still the one person whose knowledge and skill I trust without question, and I am lucky to have her as my literary agent. I am grateful to Martha Conway and her University of California, Berkeley Extension class, where I began the story that became this book. Over the three-year period I worked on the novel, I received help and inspiration from many and sometimes, I felt, from the river itself. Thanks to my husband, Larry, who encouraged me to finish the book; to my Hanford lunch group, whose support is strong after all these years; to environmental scientist Wendy Cooper, who helped me imagine Claire's job; and to my inspirational friends, Cynthia and Thane Murphy.

This book is set at and near the San Joaquin River, and for the sake of the story, I have also created a fictional river conservancy group housed first at the river and then at the university. The group has nothing in common with the very real San Joaquin River Parkway and Conservation Trust, of which I am a member. I have also changed some of the geography to aid the plot.

Thanks to the members of my literary family – Jen Badasci, Annie and John Brantingham, Hazel Dixon-Cooper, Christopher Allan Poe and Stacy Lucas – who kindly fillet my work on a weekly basis and whose input helped shape the book. I am especially grateful to Hazel, who has spent hours with me on the banks of the San Joaquin River, through every season, looking out at the water as we ask each other, 'What if?'

PROLOGUE

They found the car on Thursday.

Timothy Slates and Ramon Reyes, another landscape technician, had been out in the river in their little boat with the outboard doing cleanup work. Timothy was one of the young men Wally had mentored when he was alive. Back then, when Timothy was only seventeen, he'd seemed almost too handsome with his large dark eyes and black hair he pulled into a ponytail. Claire Barrett had watched his unchanging smile as Wally called him 'Buddy,' and patted him on the back. She had noted Timothy's halting speech. Yet in spite of or maybe because of his slow, careful manner, he had been able to land a full-time job with the river conservancy after he received his GED. Now, after Wally's death, he was acting restoration technician.

Timothy was the one who found it.

PROLOGUE

ONE

Claire

Claire would remember the moment like a snapshot, the late afternoon a cold black-and-white with just a touch of gold that lit the water. After working two weeks straight on the San Joaquin River restoration project, she and Tessa had taken off and driven to San Francisco, some three hours north. They took Highway 99 north to Manteca and then over the Bay Bridge, driving without music as they always did – no need for background noise. Tessa had been obsessed with finding the vines she had spotted online, and Claire felt the outing would be good for them. They both needed a break from the routine and the pressures of their lives – Claire's divorce, Tessa's preoccupation with Jake's going away to college.

When they returned to Fresno later that day, what little sun the afternoon had held faded into the horizon.

'All that to buy some reclaimed forty-year-old grapevines.' Tessa tugged at the blue knit cap that hid everything but her eyes and fringe of dark bangs.

'But it was fun, and you were right. It will be a good project for the schools or maybe the Green Thumbs,' Claire said. 'Besides, this is raisin country. We should have grapes in our community garden.'

Tessa shook her head. 'Eric is really going to think I'm crazy now.'

'He'll be fine.' Claire turned onto the narrow drive that led to their offices, buzzed down her window and let the river breeze blow in. 'It's not the first impulsive thing we've done.'

'Still, he's going to think it's weird.' The joy drained from Tessa's voice and she wrapped her arms around herself. 'Let's not tell him.'

Her response surprised Claire. Eric seemed preoccupied with his case. He wouldn't care how they'd spent their day.

As soon as Claire had parked, Tessa jumped out of the car, opened the back door and began unloading the vines.

Claire followed. 'I think you've had too much caffeine, Tess.'

Tessa shook her head. 'I'm all right. And these are just perfect. Wally will love them, won't he?'

'Wally?' Claire stiffened.

'Right. Wally.' She leaned into the car again and lifted out a gnarled trunk. 'You know how much he loves helping us plant the stuff we find.'

'Tessa,' Claire said. 'Wally's been dead almost three months. We went to his memorial service together.'

The smile on Tessa's face went rigid. 'Oh, that's right.' She looked away from Claire, down into the bundle of vines she held. 'Well, let's get these into the shed and pick up dinner on the way home.'

Clues had shown up earlier but Claire had ignored them. She'd explained away the forgotten appointments, the mix-ups in plans for lunch and coffee. She could not explain away this, though.

'Wait a minute.' Claire forced herself to speak slowly, without judgment. 'Wally was our friend, OK? Explain to me how you could forget he died.'

'It just slipped my mind, that's all. I remember now, though.' She seemed to shift gears and her smile became engaging, convincing. 'I'll call Eric and tell him we're on our way.'

They stopped at the market and shopped, Tessa carrying on a running monologue about the price of organic lemons and wondering aloud what would follow high-pH water as the new trend of the year. Eric had texted Tessa to say he was running late too, so he wouldn't even know that they had sneaked off on a day trip. Claire doubted he would mind. Her concern was what Tessa had said about Wally.

It didn't seem to bother her, though. As Claire drove them home from Whole Foods, Tessa made fun of the overdone Christmas decorations in front of the houses facing the river bluffs. 'The rich side of the street,' they always called it, even though Tessa lived there. If the developers had their way, the river would be a memory, and the towns of Central California, including this one, would all blend together like exits on a freeway. They would disappear into the mass of franchise restaurants and pseudo-Mediterranean shopping malls that made up Southern California. These hills and the drops to the fog-shrouded river below separated and saved them. As long as they had the wetlands, scarce and threatened as they might be, there would be no housing developments replacing the water and the city would end at the river.

Tessa pointed at an illuminated merry-go-round decoration in front of a two-story Tudor, its balcony draped with lights. 'Here we are trying to save the environment, and people are putting up garbage like that.'

She sounded like herself again. Only then did Claire realize how tightly she had been gripping the steering wheel.

'Traffic's crazy this week,' she said. 'I can pick you up for work tomorrow.'

'Eric offered to drive me.' Tessa paused. 'It's about the only time we get to be together these days. He's working on that case around the clock, and I understand. The woman's life is at stake.'

'A woman who may have murdered her husband in his sleep.' Claire spoke before she could stop herself.

'Gloria Sudbury is innocent. It was self-defense.'

'If you say so.' Claire tried to laugh it off.

'Eric says so.'

He met them in the driveway. Claire had never seen Eric McCall without a coat and tie, and tonight was no exception. His silver-gray jacket almost matched his hair. His lips pressed together in a smile she had once thought of as arrogant but now knew was a professional mask to hide his emotions from the public. Somewhere along the way, it had crept into his private life.

Few men made Claire forget how tall she was, and the fact that Eric did was due to his attitude as much as his height. He had a way of speaking, of moving, that made him look impenetrable. Now, he loomed outside the open door of the garage. If this were a courtroom, Claire would want him on her side, as he had been not long ago. When he'd walked into her divorce hearing, she'd felt the rustle of astonishment in the room. Iconic, high-fee criminal attorneys didn't usually dirty the mahogany of their lives by arguing a custody case between an environmental scientist and her ex. Yet, thanks to their friendship, Eric had insisted on handling the legal details as effortlessly as if offering to take out the trash.

'There you are,' he said to Tessa through Claire's open window. 'Hi, Claire.'

Claire stepped out and, even as she responded to his polite hug with a reciprocal squeeze, she knew she needed to go home and think about whether to tell him how concerned she was about Tessa.

'I'll bet you're wondering what happened to dinner.' Tessa lifted a bag in each hand. 'It's crab season, and these are already cracked. I bought a couple of overpriced lemons, too. And for dessert, I picked up farmhouse cheddar, apples, and what looks like a really amazing port.'

'You two enjoy,' Claire said. 'I need to get going.'

'Nonsense.' Tessa walked toward the door.

'Don't rush off,' Eric said. 'I just got here myself. Let's hit the wine and worry about food when we feel like it.'

His gaze drifted to Tessa, and Claire realized he wasn't looking at his wife in a casual way. He was studying her, his manner expectant. Tessa seemed to sense his scrutiny and turned around.

'Please stay.' Despite Tessa's smile, her voice sounded tight. She took Claire's arm. 'You're part of the family. Come on.'

As she started to protest, Eric took her other arm. 'She's right, Claire. Come inside.'

She could tell by the effortless way he moved ahead and held open the door to the house for them that he thought she was resisting because they had gone from two couples to one couple and a best friend.

'I guess I could have one glass of wine,' Claire said. 'But then, I really do need to get home.'

They walked inside, past the black-and-white tiled entry hall and its multifaceted crystal chandelier, into the living room with a forest-green velvet sofa trimmed in rosewood, matching coffee table and, above the fireplace, a framed red-and-black kimono, its stiff arms extended.

The dining room was a study in neutrals ranging from white to taupe, with an occasional green spike of a plant. They sat at the round cherry-wood table overlooking what was now the blackness of the river.

Tessa insisted on serving them. One of her many gifts included infusing a simple gathering with the energy of a party. Just the right knife, crystal glasses, paper-thin slices of roast beef, a bowl of horseradish and crème fraîche, and tart little cornichons shared an oval serving platter.

'Appetizers,' Tessa said, 'while I slice the cheddar.'

The smell of roasting garlic and the piano concerto in the background softened the formality of the room. Still wearing her blue hat, Tessa was magic. Almost forty-six, she moved like a dancer covering every undiscovered spot on the stage.

But she had forgotten that Wally had died. She had forgotten that horrible funeral service they had attended and how the two of them had agreed to sneak out early so they wouldn't have to confront the open casket.

That was why Claire hadn't wanted to come inside. It would be worse than a lie to pretend everything was fine. Although she had no idea how to do it, she had known that if she stepped into this house, she would have to talk to Eric.

'I'll be right back,' Tessa said and headed for the kitchen.

Claire looked out of the window. 'I can't believe your Meyer lemon survived the freeze.' What a clumsy beginning.

'Thanks to you for telling us what to feed it.' Eric glanced at the tree, lit by a spotlight on their patio, and bit into one of the French pickles.

'How's your case going?' she asked.

'I'm going to win, in spite of the bad press. No, because of it.' He loosened his tie, and the vulnerability in his expression made her more comfortable.

'Eric?'

He glanced at her beside him at the table. 'More wine?' he asked as his public smile returned.

'My head's already buzzing.' But she reached for her glass anyway.

'What's wrong, Claire?' His voice lowered. 'Is Danny still trying to keep Liz from you? If so, I'll kick his ass.' He laughed. 'Metaphorically, and maybe literally as well.'

'It's not that.'

'Then what?' The commanding attorney tone took over his voice. 'Tell me.'

'Do you remember Wally?'

He sighed in a way that held as much relief as anything else. 'That old restoration technician guy you and Tessa hung out with when she first started volunteering?'

Claire nodded. 'You know he died, right?'

'Of course, and not long ago.' Eric took his tie the rest of the way off and draped it over the back of his chair. 'Why would you ask me that? You and Tessa went to the memorial.'

Claire reached for her glass of wine and swallowed as much as she could.

'Except,' she finally said, 'Tessa doesn't remember.'

He seemed to freeze. 'Of course she does.'

'Well, you're right. She does when you remind her.' She reached for his arm but quickly removed her hand. 'Then she forgets. She's been forgetting other things, too.'

He got up from the table and strode toward the view that high-profile cases like the current one had paid for. When he turned to face her, she imagined herself in a courtroom.

'She's distracted. Jake just left for college. Call it the empty-nest syndrome, whatever. She's stuck in this big house without her son, and I've got to admit, I've been preoccupied with this case.'

'I understand that,' Claire said.

'Do you?'

The question echoed in her ears. He didn't have to say more. A rush of heat shot to her face at the reminder that Claire's own empty nest had not been by choice.

'I'm just trying to help, Eric. This isn't easy for me. I love Tessa.'

'So do I.' He sat down beside her again, farther away than before. 'Let's leave it at that, shall we?'

She had tried and failed. 'If that's what you want,' she said.

Tessa returned to the room. Her chili-pepper apron looked painted on her black shirt.

'Where've you been, Tess?' Eric asked. 'What took you so long? We missed you.'

She didn't seem to hear. 'I was just looking for . . .' She caught sight of the roast beef platter on the table and smiled. 'Oh, there it is.'

Eric and Claire's eyes met and, without a word, they agreed to ignore that, too.

'Sit down with us.' Eric reached for Tessa's hand. 'Come sit.'

Claire couldn't take any more. She didn't know what to do or say. 'I wish I could stay,' she said, 'but I really need to get home.'

Tessa

When Claire leaves, she takes the light with her. Part of that light is in her hair, the occasional strands of silver in her dark braid shining like the stars outside. Most of Claire's light is in her face, though, the high cheekbones and almond-shaped eyes. As dark as they are, Claire's eyes shine too.

Tessa stands at the sink and looks outside for the girl on the river. Earlier, a glint of blue flashed and then disappeared behind one of the eucalyptus trees. She looks down at the suds on her fingers as she dips a plate in the water and feels ashamed, but not sure why. Her bra strap slips down under the sleeve of her top and she doesn't bother to push it up, not with her wet hands. Her mind follows the path of the day, the long drive and curving lines of traffic, then the nursery, the vines, the greenhouse. Claire's laughter is sudden and natural now. She's no longer guarded and unfriendly the way she was when they first met. But she wasn't laughing tonight.

'Need any help?' Eric stands in the doorway. He's lost his tie but still looks professional.

'I want a Christmas tree,' she says.

'What's wrong with the one we have? I can bring it in from the garage and we can put it in the living room, the same as always.'

She closes her eyes, but all she can see in her mind is the tree down the street, all those lights.

'Tessa?' His voice is thick. 'I miss Jake, too.'

Through the windows behind him, the colors of sunset on the river blend into night.

She puts her hand on her hip, smiles and eyes him in the way she knows will get his attention.

'It's late,' he says, but moves next to her anyway, puts his arms around her.

'Finally,' Tessa whispers, and folds into him.

TWO

Claire

They did not start as friends. Their bond had nothing in common with those lifelong relationships that sometimes seem as much about habit and obligation as anything else. They had met back when both their kids were in school. Tessa had seemed one of those perfect moms who had time to head every parent event, attend every science fair, every concert. Their paths had crossed frequently when Jake and Liz, Claire's daughter, were younger, and might have stopped once they were in high school, but that's when Tessa began volunteering for the river conservancy, where Claire was an environmental scientist.

'A rich-bitch volunteer,' Rosemary called her and, although Claire knew better than to accept anything her director Rosemary Boudreaux said at face value, the woman's judgment had seeped into her own.

One afternoon, almost three years before, when Claire and Rosemary were heading back from the field, a new group of volunteers emerged from another path, where they had been planting. Once trained, they would lead field trips, work in the river store or on habitat restoration. Rosemary greeted them and then went back to her office. A former immigration attorney who'd gotten sick of fighting the system, as she put it, Rosemary dressed in blazers, regardless of the weather, and twisted her dark hair into such a severe knot that the others joked about it, saying with that hairdo she would never need Botox.

True, her job was difficult, overseeing everything from fundraising and finances to habitat restoration, invasive species removal and land-use planning. But from the beginning, Rosemary had made it clear that she thought it was a step down for her, and she openly discussed plans to start an environmental consulting firm with her longtime friend, Natalia Paden. Although Rosemary considered her leaving a threat, most of the staff members, Claire included, couldn't wait. That day, she started to follow Rosemary inside, but something made her turn around and look back at the volunteers.

Tessa, the brunette that Rosemary had labeled a rich bitch, had spotted something on the ground that made her hesitate and then kneel. Claire watched her reach down, smiling as a child would, to pick it up.

'Stop!' Claire yelled, and Tessa's hand froze in the air.

Claire's job description did not include harassing the volunteers, but she had already crossed the wide sloping area between them to where this newbie knelt.

'What's wrong?'

'Didn't they teach you anything on your orientation?' Claire said. 'Like the wild in wildflower, for instance?'

Tessa glanced down at the California jewelflower in the ground and then back up at Claire. 'I didn't pick it. See? It's alive and healthy. Breathing, even.'

Claire looked at the purple-lined white blossom and tried not to show her embarrassment. The others tittered.

These women weren't evil, Claire reminded herself as Tessa joined them again, leaving the flower unharmed. Dressed in their cashmere sweaters and equally expensive shoes, they could be doing worse things than trying to save the river. Besides, if Claire were as good with people as she was with plants, she wouldn't have been so abrupt.

'Sorry. I overreacted.' She kept her eyes on Tessa. 'Once you've been here longer, it might make sense. A wildflower can support an entire ecosystem of birds and small animals. A lot of creatures depend on blossoms like these for their food supply.'

'It does make sense.' She smiled the way she had at the flower. 'I'm glad we'll be working together, Doctor Barrett.'

'It's Claire,' she said, and put out her hand.

Tessa grinned and took it.

Rosemary had been wrong, as usual.

After that day, Claire and Tessa exchanged tentative greetings whenever they saw each other, as if sharing the secret of their shaky beginning. One early morning at the farmers' market, Claire spotted Tessa in a pair of jeans and a sloppy top that would not have survived inspection from her fashionable friends. She lifted a handful of curly kale, dropped it in her bag and then waved as Claire approached.

'It's sustainable, right?'

'I'm sure it is,' Claire told her.

'When you're finished, want to grab some coffee?'

Claire thought about it. 'I probably ought to get back home.'

'Why?' Tessa grinned.

And because Claire could think of no excuse, she said, 'Never mind. Why not?'

That was their first of a lot of great conversations, and after Tessa was promoted from volunteer to director of education, she seemed to grow more focused. She often said that their friendship brought out the rational person in her and the people person in Claire.

Now, Tessa seemed to be drifting from rational to forgetful. That morning at their office on the river, she had already forgotten to make a second pot of coffee, and the scorched smell filled the cramped quarters. Rosemary showed her disapproval by propping open the front doors despite the chill in the air.

Tessa shrugged, smiled at Claire and went outside. Claire followed.

The rainstorm that erupted that morning had blown itself out and left behind a day so clear they could see the Sierra Nevada mountains in the distance. Claire and Tessa watched a squadron of white pelicans soar toward the river. When Tessa had worked as a volunteer before Jake left for college, she'd dressed like her friends, with designer deck shoes that wouldn't have stood up to even a mild drizzle. Today she wore sunglasses, jeans, REI hiking boots like Claire's and a Gore-Tex jacket.

'No reason we should have to stay inside and smell burnt coffee,' Tessa said.

'I wish Rosemary hadn't been here to see it,' Claire told her.

'She'd hate me no matter what.'

'What happened between you two anyway?'

'I have no idea.' The busload of regulars from the adult daycare center pulled in and they walked toward it. 'I never did anything to her. Natalia hates me, too.'

Al's ex-wife. Claire felt a twinge of guilt even though she knew she shouldn't. 'Let's hope Natalia and Rosemary really do go into business together,' she said. 'In the meantime, I don't mind making the coffee.'

Tessa stopped, childlike, and her eyes grew wide. 'I won't do it again.'

'It's all right,' Claire said. 'Anyone can leave a pot on too long. Besides, that cheap stuff Rosemary makes us buy is no great loss.'

The Green Thumbs, as the group from the adult daycare center was called, got off the bus. A couple had problems negotiating the steps. The others just took their time. Tessa greeted them with hugs and smiles and, in a soft, firm voice, directed them and their caregivers to the potting table. Just like that, she was in charge again, but a moment ago she had been close to tears.

'Tessa,' Claire began.

'Later.' She motioned toward the group congregating at the wooden potting table. 'We'll catch up later.'

Just then, Rosemary came running outside, holding her phone.

'What's going on?' Claire asked her.

'It's Timothy.' She motioned out toward the water.

'Is he all right?' Claire looked out at the empty green boat floating near the shore. Timothy and Ramon, the other technician, had deserted it as they pulled something else to land.

'They just found a car out there,' Rosemary said. 'They found a car in our river.'

Most of the Green Thumbs group and Tessa drew nearer to the bank.

'Stay back,' Rosemary told them.

Claire ran to the edge of the muddy drop and saw the two men. The twisted shell they had pulled from the river was the front part of a car. For a moment, Claire felt there would be something in that car, maybe even someone. She made her way down the side of the hill to the water's edge.

The steering wheel had been broken off. One bucket seat was entirely gone, leaving only the metal frame. The other seat was ripped apart.

They stood there, deadly still. 'Is anyone in it?' Claire asked Timothy.

'No, ma'am. We had to call the sheriff, though.' In spite of the chilled air and wet clothes, his face was white. 'Doesn't look good. You can't break up a car that easy.'

'What about the registration?' Claire moved closer and stepped into the water.

'Gone.'

'It's got to have a vehicle identification number.'

'I don't think so.' He shook his head slowly at the mutilated frame.

'The VIN should be right there.' Mud sloshed against her boots as she approached the car and leaned down near the lower-left corner of what had once been the steering wheel. 'I think it's in six or seven places on a car.'

Tessa followed her into the water.

'Get back here,' Rosemary called. 'We need to wait for the sheriff.'

She was right, but Claire couldn't deal with Timothy's slow pace. She stood up and searched where the driver's-side door would be. Not enough of it was left. There was no way they could trace this vehicle, and that unnerved her. If anyone had been inside when it hit the water, they could not have survived.

'Come on back,' Rosemary called. 'The sheriff is on her way.'

'Can you tell what make it is?' Tessa asked, ignoring Rosemary.

'No.' Claire studied the remaining seat. 'Some kind of sports car, maybe? I'm not even sure if there was a back seat. See how it kind of tapers off here?'

Something glinted beneath the torn backrest of the driver's seat. Claire knelt, and the water seeped over the top of her boots. Tessa took in a sharp breath as she saw it too.

Ripples splashed behind them and Claire tried to maintain

her composure. She shuddered with the cold and for what she could see clearly now.

Rosemary's curiosity overcame her need to play director. She rolled up her jeans, which made her look ridiculous because the rest of her was perfectly dressed and made-up. 'Do you realize that we could get in serious trouble for disturbing this?' she demanded. But she was staring at the vehicle as well.

'What is that?' she asked, pointing at the seat. 'Is it a knife?'

'No.' Claire shook her head, and the frigid water numbed her feet and her legs. 'It's a gun.'

Timothy stared down at the weapon. 'Looks like a Luger.'

Tessa

Tessa listens as the sheriff, a slender but muscular woman with short brown hair, tells them what will happen next. The gun is too old to have a serial number, but they take it anyway. They will drag the river in search of a license plate, a VIN. 'Or a body,' the sheriff says, almost apologetically, as if the river is their home and she and her crew are invading it in search of the unthinkable.

Claire cringes, and Tessa realizes that she is staring at her, waiting for a reaction. Claire puts her arm around Tessa's shoulder and whispers, 'It will be all right. Let's go back now.'

'I was afraid of this,' Tessa says as she and Claire stand on the road beside the river.

'Afraid of what?' Claire asks.

'It's unnatural,' she says. 'All of this. It's wrong.' Her feet burn with cold, and she knows Claire's must, too.

Beyond them, the water catches pieces of light and gleams in the winter sun.

'Is that what's bothering you? The car?'

It would be easy to say yes, but she can't. 'There's something I haven't told you. I was afraid you'd think I was crazy.'

'You don't have to keep anything from me,' Claire says, and even though her voice is soft, Tessa senses the tension in it.

'I'm not even sure if it means anything.'

'Tell me.'

'I've been seeing things,' she says. 'At night, on the river. Eric thinks I've been having nightmares, and I let him.'

'What kind of nightmares?'

Something about the way she asks the question makes Tessa wish she hadn't brought it up, but now it's too late. Claire will dig at her words until she uncovers the truth. 'I keep seeing a girl.'

Claire doesn't move. 'A girl? Where?'

'Sometimes she's beside the water. Sometimes she seems to be on top of it. Sometimes all I can see is her face. Even though I can't see it very clearly, I know what she looks like.'

She worries that Claire might give her the fake smile of understanding she reserves for those she thinks are making stuff up or simply clueless.

Instead, Claire gently touches her arm. 'Maybe what you saw has something to do with that.' She motions toward the water, the gathered strangers, the car.

'But what if I'm wrong? What if it really is a strange kind of nightmare? Do you think I'm crazy? What if Eric does?'

'Nobody thinks you're crazy. We love you,' she says. 'This is too important to keep to yourself.'

'That's the problem. I don't know how to explain it.' Tessa turns away and goes inside to the office, with its back-window view of the river, to the small kitchen. Warm air settles on her face, but she is still cold. Claire walks up beside her. 'Coffee?' Tessa asks and then wrinkles her nose when she spots the pot no one has bothered to wash.

Claire shakes her head. 'This girl you saw. How old is she? What does she look like?'

'I might not have seen anything, Claire. You know how the moon can change the way the water looks at night.'

'Don't,' Claire says. 'Don't lie to me.'

'Saying I don't know is not a lie.' Tessa hates the feeling of being scolded. She hates feeling guilty that she can't seem to trust Claire with this. She is afraid of that look of disappointment she glimpses before Claire masks it with something pleasant and kind.

'Of course not.' Claire surveys the people removing more

of the car's warped remains from the water and hugs herself as if trying to ward off a chill. 'Just try to tell me what you saw.'

'Let me think about it, OK?'

'I'm not sure how much time we have to think about this one, Tessa.'

Claire's expression is a reminder of how much she hates it when Tessa tries to avoid dealing with crises.

'I need to put it together better in my head. Just seeing that car, the gun. It scares me.'

Claire turns her back to the window and leans against the aluminum sink. 'I have to go,' she says. 'I'm not going to pressure you. Just go ahead, give it some thought, and maybe we can talk again.' She starts to say something else but then turns and heads for the door.

Tessa glances down at her hands and realizes she has been digging her nails into her palms so hard that her flesh is criss-crossed in sharp red lines. She stands at the sink, turns on the cold water and lets it run over her hands until numbness replaces the pain. Then she remembers. The visitors from the adult daycare center.

The potting table is empty. Sandwiched by a caregiver on either side, the small group stands outside the window, facing the river like lost children.

Tessa rushes back outside.

THREE

Claire

I f Tessa had really seen someone at the river, then she may have also witnessed more than she was sharing. Something was making her disconnect from reality. Hallucination or trauma? Claire had no idea.

Going to Eric now would be a betrayal. That left Claire with only one option. Danny. Her ex-husband had a different way of communicating with Tessa. At one time, she would have told Claire anything, but now, maybe Danny could get her to talk more about this woman she thought she had seen by the river. As Claire drove, the clusters of tall palm trees became more frequent. Fresno may have been named for its ash trees, but everywhere she looked, especially out here close to the airport, she saw those Hollywood palms listing in the slightest breeze.

Claire pulled into the parking space behind his office near the airport. Nothing about it suggested that Danny chartered close to three thousand aircraft, from helicopters to jets, from his four-room structure.

'Stripped mall,' Liz used to call it when she was young and they were a family. Claire still thought of it that way, although the center now bulged with businesses quietly preparing to trail the progression to the north end of the city. That's what happened in San Joaquin Valley towns like Fresno. Each time the city expanded, each time a major shopping center lured customers farther north, local businesses deserted their old locations and did the same, following the money.

Other than Eric, Danny was the only person who knew Tessa as well as Claire did, and at times she had almost envied their ease with each other. Up until the divorce last year, the four of them had been inseparable. They had shared dinners,

attended plays, and traveled to Danny and Claire's cabin in
Wawona, at the entrance to Yosemite. In the quiet hours
between dusk and dawn, they had bragged and complained
about their kids. Now, she realized that it was the group
and not just her marriage that had made her feel secure.

The breakup had strengthened her friendship with Tessa and
Eric. They were both angry with Danny for demanding a
divorce after he received the anonymous call about Al and her
– a call Al may well have made.

As Danny packed to leave that night, he had demanded to
know how long the affair had gone on.

'It wasn't an affair,' Claire had told him as they faced each
other in their bedroom for the last time.

'Of course it was.' He'd stuffed the last shirt into his bag
and closed it. 'What kind of married woman has another man
for a best friend?'

It was a good question, and Claire hadn't been able to
answer it, not only because Danny was better at arguing than
she was, but because he had a point. There must have been
something lacking in her marriage or in herself.

Had Al been single when they met, she never would have
allowed herself to get close to him. But he was devoted to
Natalia and he had seemed safe. They had been thrown together
through his graphics work for the river conservancy, but soon
they'd found other shared interests, including his outstanding
black-and-white nature photography. When Natalia left him
abruptly, he was devastated, but nothing changed between Claire
and him. Danny had never indicated any concern until that last
night as he picked up his packed bags and glared at her.

'Lucky for Al that I got that anonymous call,' he had said
in the sarcastic tone she hated. 'Lucky that the guy who called
happened to have my number, wouldn't you say?'

'I don't know what you're talking about,' she'd said.

He'd stopped at the bedroom door. 'Just that Al won. He
can have you now, and that's what he's wanted all along.'

The conversation had shaken Claire so much that she had
avoided unnecessary contact with both Danny and Al. Now,
though, she remembered that Tessa had always said Danny
was like a brother to her.

Claire always thought of the stretch of off-ramp towns between Bakersfield to the south and Sacramento to the north as the Forgotten California. At more than 800,000 population, Fresno was still more small town than city, more pass-through place than destination. Yet this was where she had settled, where she and Danny had raised their daughter, and sometimes in the early morning, especially on a stormy day when she could inhale the scent of raindrops mixed with the wind blowing in from the river, she felt at home here and something close to happy. Since she and Danny had split – since he had left her – those moments were less frequent.

Yes, she had cheated, and she knew Danny would never do that. No, alcohol wasn't an excuse, and yes, she still cared about Al, regardless of what he might or might not have revealed to Danny.

She planned her arrival close to noon because the office would be closed, and Amanda, Danny's assistant, took her lunch break then. She probably should have called before stopping by but it was too late now. Walking unannounced through his back door made her even more uncomfortable. As usual, the place smelled of his French roast. Nothing had changed. The refrigerator's electric hum filled the room. Inside would be the usual bottles of Pellegrino and Harp Lager, never cans. Next to the sink, a meticulous countertop held a coffee pot and four mugs upside-down on a tray. The poster Liz had created for Danny in one of her art classes hung on the cupboard door. *Even Superman is Clark Kent most of the time.* Liz, who hated her now. Liz, who had said, 'You're not my mother anymore.'

In a khaki polo shirt and jeans, Danny was bent over a spreadsheet that covered most of the counter. His gray-streaked auburn hair had fallen across his forehead.

'Danny?'

He jerked upright, pushed his hair back and put on the new, friendly face he used for dealing with her now. 'Oh, Claire. Hi. You surprised me.'

'I should have called,' she said.

'You don't need to do that. I could use a break anyway.' He glanced down at her hands.

'Me too.' Claire followed his gaze, realized she was picking at her thumbnail and forced herself to stop. 'I mean, I need to talk to you about something.'

He motioned toward a stool on the other side of the worktable. 'If it's Liz, there's nothing I can do. You're her mother, and you're the only one who can make it right.'

In spite of his laidback manner, his tone was steady, too steady, an accusation.

'It's not Liz. It's Tessa, actually.'

He sighed, as if he had been holding his breath, expecting something worse. 'Is she all right?'

Claire walked around the table to the stool but couldn't make herself sit. 'She's having problems remembering things, important things, and Eric refuses to see it. He's wrapped up in that case of his.'

'Eric's always wrapped up in something.' He picked up his coffee mug, a new one, white ceramic, *Dan* in red script on the front. 'Can I get you some of this?'

She shook her head and wondered when he had changed from Danny to Dan. 'I wouldn't have bothered you but I need to talk to someone who cares about Tessa. You're her friend, too.'

'Well, it's not as if I can just mosey over to their place and ask how she's doing.' He paused as if checking to see if the barb registered.

'But you talk to her, don't you? She mentioned that you were giving Jake flying lessons.'

'That was right before he left for college. We haven't spoken much since then. She's always rushed and, to tell you the truth, I figured she was more comfortable being your friend than mine.'

'Tessa's not like that.'

'She hasn't been in a big hurry to keep in touch.'

'That's not like her either,' Claire said.

'But she is a little spacey, memory issues or not.' A plane flew over and drowned out the rest of his words.

Although Claire had once been comfortable speaking around the noise of the airport, she no longer knew how.

'True. Sometimes, she seems fine. Other times, she forgets

things. When I try to talk to her about it, she just laughs it off.'

He filled his mug and leaned against the counter. 'Are you sure there's really something wrong, or is it just Tessa being Tessa?'

'It's more than that. I tried to talk to Eric.'

'And you actually thought he would make time to care?'

His friendship with Eric was one more casualty of the divorce, and now Danny hated him almost as much as he hated Al and her.

'I know how you feel about him, all right? And instead of making snide remarks, you might consider being grateful he didn't charge us for our divorce.' Claire's burst of anger surprised her but Danny's smug expression remained the same. 'This is about Tessa,' Claire told him. 'Something's wrong, and I don't know how to help her.'

'Maybe she doesn't need help. Have you ever considered that?' He sat down across from her and glanced up at the Superman poster. 'People have good days and bad days.'

'This is more than a bad day, Danny.'

'Well, maybe something's bothering her and she just hasn't felt like talking about it with you. You're not exactly the best judge of people, you know.'

His words stung, but she shot back anyway. 'She forgot that Wally died.'

'I doubt that.'

'She did until I reminded her,' Claire said. 'Did you hear about the car that was pulled out of the river today?'

He nodded. 'I also heard about the gun.'

She took a deep breath and forced her expression to remain neutral. 'Who told you about that?'

'I don't think it's a secret that there was a German Luger in that car. We both know Al kept one in his office.'

'I'm not here about that.' Claire's voice shook. 'After the sheriff came, Tessa told me she's been seeing a girl out there. Maybe I'm not a great judge of people, but I would say that's reason for concern, wouldn't you?'

He paused and squinted at her the way he did when questioning her judgment, her reliability. 'Do you think she witnessed something out on the river? A crime of some kind?'

'I don't know, Danny, but I need your take on this. Will you talk to her? Try to get her to tell you what she's seen?'

'I guess I'd better.' He set his mug on the table. 'I didn't realize . . . I mean, I thought maybe you were overreacting.'

'When have I ever overreacted about anything?'

'OK.' He put up a hand. 'I hear you.'

'I wouldn't have come here if I had any choice,' she said.

He winced. 'You make yourself very clear. And you're right. She's my friend, too. I'll let you know what happens when I talk to her.'

'That's all I ask, Danny.' Claire knew she could depend on him for this, even though they were no longer together and even though she could barely remember how that felt. She could depend on him for honesty.

The back door opened and Amanda stepped inside, high-lighted hair pulled up in a ponytail, skin-tight red pants. Red.

'Lunch is served,' she chirped. 'Two panini sandwiches, and yes, Dan, yours is the sourdough.' She glanced over at Claire as if seeing her for the first time. 'Hey, hon. Want to join us? These things are huge.'

'No, thanks. I was just leaving.' The facade of friendship, of casual coffee, could last only so long. Claire bolted for the door. 'Let's talk later, Danny. I need to get back.'

'Hold on a minute.'

'No, I need to go.'

He followed her outside, right under the blast of a jet taking off.

'Now what's wrong?' he shouted over the noise. 'I told you I'd call Tessa and try to figure out what's going on with her.'

'I appreciate it.' The plane shot into the sky, leaving the parking lot silent again. Claire reached for her car door.

His hand stopped her. 'I just asked you what's wrong.'

'I don't want an argument, but come on, Danny. Amanda sure as hell hasn't wasted any time.'

'You have some nerve.' He stepped away from her. 'It's a fucking sandwich! The last time I checked, you were the one who cheated on me.'

Claire exhaled, her breath steady now. He'd finally said what he'd wanted to since he'd looked up from his spreadsheet and saw her standing there.

'Goodbye, Danny.' Claire climbed into her car without another word.

Tessa

Tessa sits on the balcony. It's cold but peaceful and she's glad she's here, away from the office with the sheriff's deputies and their questions, away from Timothy's frightened eyes. Poor Timothy. All he did was find the car, but he will worry that he's going to get blamed for whatever happened to it.

The surface of the river, dark as it is, has faces etched on it. A woman's face, a girl's, with eyes as pale and endless as the sky. Tessa squints and searches for the ice-blue dress and thinks she catches a glimpse of it. Something out there is blue, that's for sure.

She hears the French doors behind her open. 'What are you doing out here?' Eric asks. 'And with no shoes?'

'Just getting some fresh air. You're home early.'

'Actually, I've been here for almost an hour. I wanted to surprise you.'

'With what?' She jumps up from the wooden bench. The redwood deck might as well be covered with ice. It's that cold. Her feet burn and then go numb.

'Come on.' Eric puts out his arms. 'Let me carry you.'

'I can walk.'

'But you don't need to when you have me.' He lowers his arms, picks her up and she settles against him. It's nice like this, safe, riding back to the warmth of indoors, hanging onto him and his scratchy jacket against her cheek.

Once inside, he lowers her to the floor. 'Well?' he says, and then she sees it.

Someone – Eric – has put up a Christmas tree so tall it almost touches the ceiling. Tiny lights blink silently.

'Oh, Eric. It's beautiful.' For a moment, she's forgotten what day it is, what month. 'And it's so tall. It must be ten feet. What a perfect surprise. Where did you find it?'

'That's my secret.' His eyes change, but before she can try to figure out what he's feeling, he pulls her to him. 'I wanted you to have the best tree, Tess.'

She wraps her arms around his neck and says, 'Looks like I do.'

Yet there is something wrong about the tree. Something familiar and very wrong.

FOUR

Claire

S o Danny knew about the gun in the car. Claire wasn't
sure how. When she asked Tessa the next morning about
the woman she had seen on the river, Tessa pretended
she didn't understand. Claire hoped Danny would have better
luck, but she no longer trusted him the way she once had. She
couldn't shake the image of the gun in that car. The shock of
seeing it had made her too tough on Tessa, who needed understanding and support more than pressure and recrimination.
Claire had seen a gun like that only once, two years ago, when
she, Tessa and Wally had helped Al Paden move his office to
downtown Fresno.

With the German Luger now in the possession of the
sheriff's department, Claire had to decide whether or not to
talk to Al. As much as she wanted him to prove to her that it
wasn't his, she knew that seeing him again was dangerous. In
spite of their time apart, their connection – at least, her
connection to him – was strong.

She still remembered how, after they finished moving some
supplies into his office one night, Al had insisted on walking
her to her car even though it was parked right outside. He had
stood on the sidewalk and watched her as she drove away.
They hadn't even touched, yet seeing him in her rearview
mirror had made her feel safe, and the sensation had warmed
her all the way home. That sense of security had probably
contributed to what happened later.

Even now, she replayed that night in her mind. It was the
biggest risk she had taken with her personal life, and that risk
had destroyed her marriage and alienated her daughter. The
price had been too great.

As Claire sat at her desk that day, she kept thinking about
the gun, thinking about Al and how easy they had once been

with each other. Back then, both of them were committed to breathing life into Fresno's struggling downtown by convincing enough business owners to leave the north part of the town and relocate there. They had hammered, painted and picked out dark-walnut planks for the floor. Al had been married to Natalia then. Their wedding photo sat on his desk upstairs, a reminder that the close conversations and even the beer or two Claire and Al drank after work were innocent because Al was as married as she was.

'I'm not a gun person,' Al had told her one night, and put an antique black-and-gold box on the partially renovated front counter. 'But there have been too many robberies down here lately.'

'You didn't buy a gun?' she'd asked.

'No. Although they're easy enough to get, legally or otherwise.' He'd opened the box. 'This was my grandfather's,' he'd told her. 'A souvenir from the war.'

Claire had stood next to him and looked down at a German Luger. Even then, its intrusion into his office had filled her with dread.

'Does it still work?'

'Oh, yes.'

'Well, just be careful,' she'd said.

Al had put the gun in his safe, and she had forgotten about it until Timothy and Ramon pulled the car out of the river and she'd spotted the gun inside it.

Claire walked to the front of the office and watched the sheriff's deputies getting ready to drag the river. Maybe it wasn't Al's gun but, either way, she had to warn him. Besides, they needed to meet face-to-face sooner or later. At least then her stomach wouldn't lurch each time she caught sight of someone who resembled him. Sometimes, during the most mundane chore, she would look up from, say, the produce aisle of the grocery store, or at the gym, and think she'd spotted him. She would force herself to look away until her breathing calmed and the wiry, sandy-haired man she thought was Al disappeared.

Rosemary drove up, parked and, on her way to the office, stopped to talk to one of the deputies. Even though she was slender, Rosemary always looked burdened, and Claire wondered with what. She seemed weighed down – with hair, with jackets and scarves, with jewelry. Today it was a gray hat, probably intended to protect her from the rain, and a matching scarf wrapped twice around her neck.

Leaving the deputy, she hurried inside. Claire turned away from the window, took one look at her expression and felt her stomach tighten. Rosemary was flushed, her smile tight. That always meant bad news she could hardly wait to share.

'I just heard more about the car,' she told Claire. 'They found bloodstains in it.'

OK, so now she did have to talk to Al. 'Human bloodstains?' she asked. 'Have they been able to tell how long they've been there?'

'That's all I know.' She shuddered. 'It's creepy. I'll be glad when we move our offices to the university.'

'Me too,' Claire said. 'I need to leave now. We have a graphics pick-up at Paden's. Our holiday fundraiser brochures are ready.'

Rosemary stepped back, unable to conceal her surprise. 'Hasn't Tessa been picking up our graphics?'

'She has a meeting,'

Rosemary glanced at the clock. 'So you have time to drive all the way downtown?'

'I do. Besides . . .' She gestured toward the river. 'I could use some time away from this.'

'We do need those brochures by tomorrow,' Rosemary said.

'I'll get them.' She buttoned her jacket. 'Could you have someone let him know I'm on my way?'

'Him?' Rosemary's thin, heavily glossed lips pressed together. 'I'm not sure Al is there but someone will be.'

Claire felt herself flush. Rosemary had probably heard the rumors about Al and her, but the older woman's strictly business expression didn't offer a clue.

On the way to his office, she drove through a cloudburst. Even with her window up, she could smell the rain. As she turned off Highway 99 and made her way through the maze of streets, she thought about what she would say to him. In order to talk to him about the gun, she would have to ignore everything else that had happened between them, and she would have to put aside the very real possibility that he might be the person who'd made the anonymous call to Danny.

The Al she had known was soft-spoken, firm but not defiant, approachable but not aggressive. The Al in her head frightened her. But it wasn't fear that kept her from seeing him. Even now, the shame and remorse felt raw.

On the west side of town in a newly renovated urban area, she parked in one of the slanted vertical spaces outside his brick-front office. *Paden Design* read the gold stenciling on the front windows.

Claire opened the door and jumped out of the car. The raindrops hit her like flecks of ice, and she ducked her head as she ran to the entrance, yanking the glass door open and shutting it quickly behind her.

She saw Al standing at the side window. He had watched her run inside, had probably seen her worried expression. He, on the other hand, appeared as relaxed as always. His heavy-rimmed glasses only seemed to brighten the humor in his eyes.

'Hi, Al,' she said, a little breathless.

'Hey.' He walked across to the counter until they were only a few inches apart. 'It's really coming down out there.'

'We need it,' they said, almost in unison.

She forced a laugh. 'The rain mantra of the San Joaquin Valley.'

'At least it's true,' he said. 'We really do need it.'

This was easy. Claire shouldn't have feared seeing him all these months.

She motioned to the bulky envelope. 'Are these our brochures?'

He nodded and folded his hands on the counter. 'I have to say I'd almost given up hope that you'd come for them in person.'

'I came because I need to ask you something,' she said. 'Well, to tell you something, actually.' The nervousness returned, and she didn't know how to continue. 'They found a car in the river.'

'I heard about it on the news.' He took a step back and seemed to study her. 'And you came down here to tell me that?'

'There's more,' she said. 'Remember a couple of years ago when we helped you move your office?'

'Of course.' His voice took on an edge she hadn't noticed before. 'Why?'

'The neighborhood was dangerous. The Glover kid and his friends even broke in here last year. The liquor store down the street got held up every few weeks.'

'I don't get it,' he said.

'There was a gun under the seat of the car they found. It looked like yours.' As she pictured the long barrel, Timothy's words returned to her. *Looks like a Luger.*

'A gun?' The breath seemed to hiss out of him. 'I haven't as much as looked at mine since we moved.'

'So it's still in your floor safe under the staircase?'

'Yeah, of course.' He glanced back at the stairs. 'Why wouldn't it be?'

'Would you mind showing it to me?' she asked.

'I'm not going to show you anything, Claire.' He pushed the brochures across the counter. 'I thought you were coming to talk about something important.'

'This is important. Why can't you just check to see where the gun is? Why are you so angry?'

'Because I've done everything I can to see you for the last six months, and you show up now only because you think my grandfather's German Luger somehow ended up in the river.'

'Al,' she said, 'I hope it's not the same one. But if it is, we need to know that. You do. I just heard that the sheriff's department found bloodstains in the car as well.'

They watched each other for a moment, Claire ready to do whatever it took to see if the gun was still where he said it was.

'Do you still leave the safe open during the day?' She took a step toward it.

'No, but I can't remember the last time I locked it.' He moved in front of her. 'There's nothing of value in there. I keep everything else upstairs.'

'But your grandfather's gun is still down here?'

'I never bothered to move it.' He turned abruptly. 'OK. Since you're so insistent, let's go take a look.'

He went under the stairs and knelt beside the unlocked safe, pulled open the door and yanked out an accordion file. 'Tax returns,' he said. 'Box of bullets. And my grandfather's German Luger.' He lifted the ornate box, placed it on the floor, opened it and stared at its contents. Claire didn't have to ask what was wrong.

'It's not here,' he said slowly. He picked up a small red cardboard box and then looked inside the safe again. 'And now there's only one box of bullets. I had two.'

'You didn't know they were missing?'

'I never even look at this.' He rose to his feet.

'I think it was your gun they found,' she said. 'How could it have gotten there?'

'Maybe when those kids broke in here and took the money?' He walked to the front again. 'I didn't even know it was gone.'

'You probably should contact the sheriff.' Claire stopped at the wood-grain countertop, one of the building's original pieces he had restored. 'You have nothing to hide, right?'

'No. Of course not.' He stared at the box of bullets in his hand and then at her. 'You could have called to tell me this.'

'I thought about it.'

'So why did you come in person when you do everything you can to avoid me?'

'I don't know.' She picked up the package of brochures and held them against her chest. 'It was a bad idea.'

'So that's it?' he asked.

She nodded.

As she neared the door, he moved ahead and stopped so that she had to look into his eyes.

'You didn't give me a chance to say this before,' he told her. 'I wasn't the one who called Danny.'

'I never said you were.' She tried to keep her breathing even and easy. 'All Danny would say is that it was a man.'

'A man who sounded like me.' He pressed his back against the doorframe. 'I wouldn't have said anything to him or anyone. Whatever happened with you two was your business. I told you so that night.'

The night that had ruined her marriage.

'I don't want to talk about it.' She reached past him for the door handle. 'And I really need to leave now.'

He didn't move and didn't attempt to stop her either. 'You and I were friends once,' he said. 'Remember?'

'We're still friends.'

'If that's the way you want it.' He opened the door and, clutching the package, Claire rushed back into the storm.

At the River
November

It's quiet out here on the river bluffs with no one around and only the flutter of wind through the trees. Not dangerous, though. Nothing out here beyond the city is dangerous.

In one of the houses in the cul-de-sac, someone is trying to hold onto summer, and the smoke from a barbecue puts a pleasant sting in the air. Follow the scent and she would find a couple of steaks on a grill, a bottle of black-red zinfandel on a patio table and two people who have found the comfort of routine gazing out at the view as they toast the end of another week.

'One day,' she says to the house, and lifts her hand out of the open window as if holding a glass of her own. 'One day, I'll be there.'

She has rehearsed this event, including questions and answers, timed it right down to twelve minutes. Then fourteen minutes on Herndon to the Highway 99 on-ramp, where she will drive away for as long as it takes to begin her new life. This decision, this meeting will only hasten the inevitable. And it's worth any unpleasantness she has to endure. It's worth even the occasional twinge of guilt.

Something makes a scratching sound on the top of her car. Just the wind, that's all. This is no slasher film, no campfire story, no leftover Halloween nightmare. This is a well-lit neighborhood and fear is a commodity she cannot afford.

The gun sits beside her. She picks it up and slides it beneath her seat. Not that she would use it. Not that she would ever use it.

There is still time to leave, to reverse this soon-to-be

irrevocable decision to destroy a marriage. Sensible people would. Sensible people would not have started.

Headlights sweep around a corner. Yes. Finally.

The car moves past. Still time. There's still time to change it. There is a knock on the window on the passenger side and her chest tightens. It will be OK. It must be.

'The door is unlocked.' It clicks and then opens slowly, with uncertainty. 'Where's your car?'

'What does it matter?'

Ten minutes, including questions. The clock is ticking.

'It doesn't,' she says. 'Let's get this over with.'

'We can't stay here. Someone might see us. Where can we go?'

Time, still time. But of course there isn't. It is happening now, the big gamble, the big everything. No point in stringing this out longer than it must be.

She starts the car and says, 'The river.'

FIVE

Claire

The day after the news of blood in the car spread, many residents, including those in relatively safe northwest Fresno, seemed to share the same fears. They imagined screams from the river, saw images of people in their backyards. That car, what was left of it, the gun and the blood, shattered the feeling of safety that had always seemed part of the bluffs of the San Joaquin River. Claire was afraid, too. She worried about Al's missing gun and Tessa's strange behavior.

She should drop it, Claire knew. It was none of her business what had happened to Al's gun. Yet she needed to know. She needed him to be telling her the truth. Claire stared out of the window of the upstairs office, watching the still, gray water beyond the parking lot. Not many people came out this way, thanks to Winston, the nasty owner of the driving range at the end of the road and his no-trespassing policy. But farther west, beside Tessa's house, it wasn't unusual to see someone jogging or parked overlooking the river. Judging from the graffiti along the cement overpass where the train crossed, there were also people no one had ever seen out here.

Last year, Bobby Glover's teenage son and some of his friends had burglarized Al's shop along with several other businesses during a downtown art festival Bobby's TV station had sponsored. As soon as the kids were caught, they'd admitted the crime and turned over the cash. If they had taken Al's gun as well, maybe that had something to do with how it got into the car.

'I'm glad I'm not the only absentminded one around here.' Tessa joined her at the front window of their office. 'I just asked if you wanted to go with us to Bobby Glover's holiday party.'

Although her tone was cheerful and relaxed, she twisted the ring on her finger and Claire noticed that Tessa's nails were ragged and bitten.

'I was just thinking,' she said. 'Actually, I was thinking about Bobby Glover Junior. Remember when he broke into Al's shop?'

'Of course,' she answered too quickly, and Claire wondered if she really did remember.

'Al got his money back, but not his grandfather's Luger.'

Tessa shoved her hands in her pockets. 'Bobby's kid took the gun?'

'Bobby and his friends, yeah. They could have,' she said.

'But you don't really know that, do you?'

'I don't know that they didn't.' It came out harsher than Claire intended.

Tessa reached for her water bottle on the table beside them and took a drink. 'Even if it's Al's gun, that doesn't necessarily mean he's guilty of anything.'

'Tell that to the sheriff's deputies.' Claire pointed at the car along the bluffs. 'They're all over the place.'

'I just wonder . . .' Tessa put the bottle back on the table. 'Your interest in this is personal, I take it.'

'Of course it's personal.' Claire fought to find her scientist voice – analytical, dispassionate. 'He was my friend before he was anything else. I thought he was your friend, too.'

'Oh, he was. He is. But that doesn't mean he's telling the truth.'

'If those kids stole his gun, it does,' Claire said.

'And you think they had something to do with the car?' Tessa shook her head slowly as if contemplating what Claire was saying. 'They're not bad kids. I don't think they've been in trouble before or since.'

'Well, they were bad that night,' Claire said. 'They were looking for money. Maybe they did steal the gun. Maybe they sold it.'

'But where? And how could we ever find out?' She looked through the window to the river, where Timothy was guiding his boat away from the bluffs. Then she remembered Jack, Timothy's brother-in-law, who bought and sold guns.

'What about Jack Byrne?' she asked. 'Maybe the kids tried to sell the gun to him. Does Timothy still live with his sister and Jack at the beagle rescue?'

'I think so. Ginger's her name, and I know Timothy helps her with the dogs.' Tessa turned away from the view and crossed her arms over her chest. 'Do you really think Jack would talk to you?'

'He might,' Claire said. 'He's always been friendly enough.'

Tessa started to speak and then bit her lip.

'What?' Claire asked.

'I don't know.' She walked over to the door and paused with her hand on the knob. 'Maybe you should just let Al fight his own battles.'

'I'm sure he is doing just that,' Claire told her, holding back her irritation. Then she guessed why Tessa was opposed to her visiting Jack Byrne. 'I get that Bobby Glover and Eric are best friends, but Bobby Junior did admit to those burglaries, and I need to know if he and his friends took Al's Luger.'

Tessa stopped at the door. 'Even if he did, do you think Jack will tell you that?'

'Again, he might.'

Timothy's little boat neared the shore.

'Good luck,' Tessa said, and drifted out of the door toward him.

Claire watched her through the window as she waved and ran out to the bluffs as if she had already forgotten their argument.

Jack Byrne had gotten to know them when he picked up Timothy's check sometimes on his day off. A muscular, friendly Boston native, Jack owned a small gun store in a strip mall that housed a smoke shop, a bank, a Mexican restaurant and a liquor store. He also helped his wife Ginger, Timothy's sister, run a beagle rescue on the west side of the river, past the railroad tracks.

At one time, Claire would have asked Tessa to come with her to talk to him. But she was going alone now. Finding a parking place was easy that early in the morning. Jack was whistling and polishing the glass cabinets when she came in the door.

When he saw her, he turned.

'Hey, Jack.'

Nothing about him, except perhaps the set of his jaw, suggested his military background.

'Hey, lady,' he said in the Boston accent he had never lost. 'What are you doing here?' He squinted at her. 'Everything OK? Timmy hasn't done anything, has he?'

'He's fine.' She approached the counter that stretched across the width of the room. Only a small swinging door separated the two of them.

'What can I do for you, Claire?' he asked her. 'You need a gun?'

'In a way.' She tried to laugh but she wasn't able to pull it off, and she knew she probably sounded as if she were choking. 'Actually, I need to *ask* you about a gun, maybe one that someone tried to sell to you.'

'People try to sell firearms to me all the time.' He walked around the counter, through the doors and stood beside her. 'What's going on? It's not Timmy?'

'No, no. I told you that.' At close range, his eyes were so pale yet so intense that her impulse was to turn away. 'I'm looking for a German Luger.'

'Consider it done.' He ducked back through the doors and started tapping information into his computer. 'Not that bad, really, considering they're historical relics. This one . . .' He turned the screen to face her. 'You could probably pick it up for about four hundred, maybe a lot less.'

'I'm not trying to buy one.' She leaned against the counter. 'I'm trying to find out if anyone tried to sell you one.'

'Why would anyone do that?' He squinted at her as if trying to figure out where this conversation was leading.

'There was a robbery downtown last year,' she said. 'A friend of mine lost some money and maybe his grandfather's Luger.'

'I heard about that.' He moved away from the computer. 'The robbery, anyway. But with all due respect, Claire, if I was going to buy stolen guns, I sure as hell wouldn't be stupid enough to admit it.'

'Maybe you didn't know it was stolen,' she said.

'Doesn't matter.' He picked up his polishing cloth again. 'Because no one has tried to sell me a gun like that.'

She knew he wanted her to leave but she couldn't seem to move. 'It's really important.'

'I'm sorry.' His voice was flat. 'I can't tell you it happened if it didn't.'

'I understand.' She started to turn, and then said, 'Is there anyone else in town, another business, where someone might go to if they wanted to sell a gun?'

'Around here?' He rubbed his chin and then looked at her. 'Around here, I'm it. I pay the best prices and I treat people right. You said that *maybe* they took your friend's Luger.'

'That's right.'

'So.' He moved toward the glass cabinet he had been polishing but kept his gaze on her. 'Maybe they didn't.'

'Right.' She nodded. 'Maybe they didn't.'

'See you later,' he said as she reached for the door. 'Let me know if I can ever be of service to you, and tell that brother-in-law of mine to behave himself.'

Claire didn't know whether or not she should believe Jack. He had a point, after all. If he were buying stolen guns he couldn't be advertising the fact.

Tessa seemed more alert the next day. Regardless of how preoccupied she was, she came alive when visitors were there, or when she did her school presentations. Although Rosemary had fought promoting her from head volunteer to education coordinator, Claire knew that, even now, Tessa was excellent at her job.

Planting season started in the wintertime, and this winter had been too warm in spite of the rain. The San Joaquin Valley, the center of agriculture for the state, needed a way out of the drought and the politicians vacillated, as always. Despite that, a few desperate plum blossoms had already squeezed out on the dark branches, their petals luminous and fragile as capiz shells.

After they stopped planting and broke for lunch, Claire took a walk with Tessa along the river bluffs. To their right, she glimpsed the blue-gray water through a tangle of trees, where Timothy and Ramon were busy in a small rowboat.

Tessa stopped to watch them. 'Did you talk to Al about his gun?'

'Not yet.' Once the lie slipped out, she was stuck with it. 'I did visit Jack's shop. He said no one tried to sell him a German Luger.'

Tessa pulled on a pair of gloves. 'Do you think it really is Al's gun?'

'I think that's a fair assumption.' She should leave it there, a simple statement, no emotion. 'I don't think he had anything to do with it getting there, though.'

'And what about the blood? Will they try to find out if it's his?'

'I doubt it.'

Claire hadn't thought about that, but there was no reason to connect Al to the blood. There wasn't even a body. 'This might not even be a crime,' she said.

Tessa seemed to drift off, watching the water, and Claire wondered if she was seeing the girl again. If so, that would mean the vision was in Tessa's mind, and Claire would be able to relax a little.

To their left, fences posted with crude, hand-painted no-trespassing signs spoiled the view. At the end of the road, a small driving range passed itself off as a golf course. They always turned back before they got there, and yet Winston continued to accuse them of trespassing.

'Is that a bluebird?' Tessa pointed to a shape on a thin wire.

'Not this early. Probably a mourning dove.' The bird spread its wings. 'Hey, you're right. It is a bluebird.'

'Good omen,' Tessa said, and kept walking toward the clubhouse.

Claire pulled her vest tighter.

'Cold?' Tessa asked.

'I'm OK.'

The changes in weather were subtle that day but Claire had dressed for them. She wore her vest over a long-sleeve T-shirt Liz had bought at a Pink concert. Weatherproof, if not glamorous, she thought. Just then, she remembered Amanda in her tight red pants.

'What's the matter?' Tessa asked.

'Danny's assistant is already hitting on him.'

'Oh, God. She's young enough to be . . .' Tessa took in a sharp breath. 'That's disgusting.'

'It doesn't matter. I need to talk to you about something else.'

'It does matter, Claire.' Tessa grabbed her arm. 'You're barely divorced.'

'Divorced is divorced,' she said. 'There's no barely, and Danny can do anything he chooses to. I did, after all.'

Just then, a tan-colored SUV pulled up beside them. She knew this car, always going way over the speed limit, was Winston's. As always, he would tell them they weren't allowed on this road. As always, they would continue walking anyway. Last week, he had chased off several of the college volunteers, telling them he would have them put in jail if they returned.

They started to move around the SUV, and then Winston lowered his window. 'Good morning, ladies. Are you aware this is private property?'

'No, it's not,' Claire said. 'We've had this conversation before and nothing's changed.'

'I don't remember any conversation. I just want you to get off this road.'

'You do remember,' she said. 'And you know we have every right to be here.'

A baseball cap hid most of his fleshy face. He took off his dark glasses and squinted at her. 'You have any ID?'

'We don't need ID to take a walk. As we've already told you, this path belongs to the state.'

'Actually, it belongs to me,' he said. 'I signed an agreement with the state four years ago. As I've told everyone who's tried to violate that agreement in the past, I own the golf course and the driving range down there.'

'I understand that,' Claire said, 'but you do not own this road that *leads* to the golf course, so if you don't mind, we are going to continue our walk now. We'll turn around before we get to your property, as we always do.'

'I said I have the right to the road.' His jowls seemed to puff up, making Claire think of a frog. 'The next time you're here, I'll have security remove you.'

'Security?' she asked. 'You mean our security people? I doubt it.'

'I've hired private help,' he said. 'Clearly your people have their hands full.'

'You can have all the help you want at the golf course, but you cannot patrol this road.'

'Watch me.' He smiled. 'And my guards, unlike those boys working for you, will be armed.'

'That's ridiculous,' Tessa said.

'You'll think otherwise if you trespass on my road again.'

Tessa stepped up to the SUV's open window. 'Why do you care who walks down to your golf course?' she snapped.

He shoved back his cap and Claire could see the glistening beads of sweat caught in the deep lines of his forehead. 'Can you imagine what would happen if anyone in this town could come out here?' He grimaced. 'We'd have to deal with trash, put in restrooms. My members pay for all this.'

'They're just dicks with sticks.' Tessa laughed and Claire's cheeks burned. Tessa was not crude, and she never acted or spoke like this.

The guy's face looked as red as Claire's must have been. 'You ladies ever try coming down here again,' he said, 'and I will not be responsible for what happens to you.'

'I'll bet you never even look at this view.' Tessa gestured to the hushed water below them, the crisscrossed branches. 'Dicks with sticks!' she shouted at him.

'You're sick,' he said. 'Disturbed. Rosemary Boudreaux needs to know about the way you two women are acting out here.'

'Need her phone number?' Tessa asked.

'Let's go.' Claire touched her arm. 'Don't let him ruin our morning.'

He gunned his engine.

'Watch that speed limit,' Tessa said, and the SUV burst down the road.

They watched him drive away.

'You know he'll complain to Rosemary,' Claire said.

'Let him.' Tessa's eyes sparkled as if the outburst had energized her. 'Shall we finish our walk?'

'We should probably get back.'

'Let's do something, Claire. That guy should not decide who gets to be out here. Let's fight him.'

She was right, and maybe a good battle with Winston was what they both needed right now. Still, Tessa's outburst was entirely out of character, more manic than angry.

'Well,' Tessa asked, 'are you on board?'

'I guess so,' Claire said.

The flush on Tessa's cheeks deepened. 'I asked if you were on board. Yes or no, Claire?'

'On board to fight Winston?' she said. 'To keep this road open to anyone who wants to walk it? Of course, I'm on board for that.'

'Good. Then let's get started.'

As they turned around and walked back, neither of them spoke. In the past, Claire would have come up with a game plan for defeating Winston and shared it with Tessa. Before, Claire would have confessed to her that she still had feelings for Al, and that she wanted to find out the truth about the gun and everything else connected to that car and that river. But she couldn't share any of that with Tessa now, and not because she didn't trust her. Because, she'd admit it, something had changed between them. She and Tessa were on opposite ends of some kind of crazy teeter-totter, and Claire was afraid what would happen if she just got up and walked away, leaving Tessa in the air to fend for herself.

Tessa

Tessa used to simply look out on this river. It used to be just the view from her window, now it's her second home. She recognizes the screech of the owl and the flapping of a beaver tail on the water. She knows where on the trail a rabbit crosses and where a squirrel stands still and blends into the colors of the tree beside it. Claire has shown Tessa this world, and sometimes it feels like the only world she has.

Today, she talked to a class of school kids about the river. Although she used a flipchart, she didn't need it. The San Joaquin River, she told them, flowed from the Sierra Nevada mountain range on its final destination to the San Francisco Bay and the Pacific Ocean. From the bluffs of this office where she and Claire worked, it moved a mile west, along the back-yards of the residential streets. She didn't tell them that it was an upscale neighborhood, nor did she say she lived there. She did explain that below the railroad tracks, just a few feet farther west, it narrowed as it moved past the beagle shelter, a scattering of country stores and finally only farmland.

The kids from the school leave dirty and satisfied. She knows how do to this, to schedule the buses, to walk into classrooms with snakes and native plants or welcome the kids out here and speak about restoration and protecting the environment. That is her strength – organization. She keeps the same notebook she always has, but now it is more detailed, more comforting.

She opens it for a glimpse of what she has written.

Wally, landscaper, our friend. Died.

Christmas tree. Not new. Now in living room.

Claire.

Claire.

Claire.

Who is the girl on the river?

SIX

Claire

Tessa had seemed to bounce back as they launched their war with Winston, the driving-range owner. She made phone calls and researched his agreement with the state. Just as they suspected, he leased the property and the lease would be up for renewal in the spring. And he did *not* own the road. He didn't even lease it. As Tessa worked to organize a protest, she stared out at the river less frequently and she didn't seem as forgetful as before.

Claire watched her carefully. Although she had hoped she could count on Danny's opinion, after the scene at his office – not to mention Amanda – she didn't want to follow up. And Eric was definitely in denial. Tessa's friendship, her insistence on living well and laughing no matter what, had gotten Claire through her divorce this past year. Tessa had even tried to convince Liz to reconcile with Claire. Even though Liz was too angry about the divorce to take that advice, Tessa had tried her best, and now Claire needed to be there for her. A scientist would demand proof of her claims, but some truths took time to prove. Unlikely as it was, Tessa might have seen a woman or girl on the river. She might have seen something to explain that car and the blood in it.

Bobby Glover was hosting his TV station's annual holiday party later in the evening. At one time, they would have attended as two couples, and Eric would never think of leaving her out just because Danny was no longer part of the picture.

Before her friendship with Tessa, Claire had known mostly other scientists. Like her parents and her brother, they were more interested in their jobs than in interacting with people. Claire still didn't relish the idea of making small talk with strangers, and it had been an emotional week. Eric would keep his eye on Tessa. Claire didn't need to be there.

Tessa brought it up as they closed up the greenhouses that Friday night. The third and largest was always the last because it was the farthest from their office.

Water was trickling into the sink and Tessa turned it off. 'Please change your mind and come with us,' she said. 'Almost everyone who attends these things is drunk and boring. I can deal with either one but not both of them together.'

'I just want to go home,' Claire told her.

'You don't have to stay long.' Tessa's voice broke. 'Please.'

She and Eric rarely asked Claire for anything. If Tessa were that uneasy, Claire couldn't turn her down.

'OK,' she said. 'I'll go.'

Tessa lifted the snakes, Colby and Roscoe, from their crates on the table back into their cage for the night. They slinked toward the shadows and, as Tessa clicked their cage door into place, Claire shuddered.

Yes, she was afraid of snakes. Surely she wasn't the only scientist who had that fear, and besides, she could fake it when she had to. Harmless as they were, the mottled yellow boa and black gopher snake still made her uneasy, and she was glad Tessa handled them in the presentations.

A phony, Danny had accused her the day he moved out. *A fake.* 'You're too spineless to stand up to your parents and tell them you'll pick your own career,' he had said. 'You pretended to be friends with Al but you couldn't wait until he and Natalia broke up.'

'That's not true,' she had told him. 'Al loved Natalia. He suffered when she left, and I suffered for him.'

She had wanted to say more to defend herself, but Danny had slammed the door and left the house with his accusations ringing in her ears. As she and Tessa now gathered their things to leave the office, she tried to tell herself that Danny had only been trying to hurt her. The cage door clicked again.

Tessa shrugged and walked toward the exit. 'Let's get out of here,' she said. 'Eric wants to get to the party early so we can leave early, too.'

'We still need to check everything.' Claire stared in the direction of the click.

One of the cage doors opened slowly.

'Tessa,' Claire said, and ran to close the door.

As she did, the thick, colorless snake known as Colby inched out of the nearest one.

'Tessa,' she said again. 'Hurry.'

Now, the door to the cage stood open.

'Colby,' Tessa scolded. 'Get back in there.'

She went back to the cage. 'Sorry,' she told Claire.

'It's OK. Just get him back in there.'

Tessa tugged at the cage, lifted the snake back into it, made a show of shutting and locking the door properly and looked up at Claire as if for approval. 'We're good to leave now, right?'

'Would you be upset if I didn't go?' Claire asked.

'You can't back out now.' Tessa glared at her. 'Eric wants everything to be the same as always.' Her voice dropped close to a whisper.

'But it's not the same,' Claire said.

'That doesn't change what Eric wants.'

'What do you mean?'

'I told you. He wants everything to be the same.' She started crying, dug a tissue out of her pocket and wiped her eyes. 'I'm so sorry. I don't know what's wrong with me.'

'There's nothing wrong with you.' Claire put her hand on Tessa's shoulder. 'You're just tired. We're all pretty rattled.'

'Don't tell Eric.' Tessa wadded the tissue in her hand. 'About this, I mean.'

'Why would I?'

'I don't know. Just don't tell him.' They closed the greenhouse, bolted the gate and walked down the path through the dusk light to the parking lot.

At the end of the driveway, Eric sat behind the wheel of his black BMW scribbling on a legal pad. The overhead light emphasized his high forehead and the intensity of his expression.

He frequently explained that he got the car as partial payment from a client who owned a dealership. Claire wasn't sure if that was because he was ashamed of driving such an expensive vehicle or if he liked pointing out his high fees in such a literal way. He looked up as they approached, got out of the car, hugged Tessa and then Claire. In the black suit and gray tie so understated that it conveyed only that it must have cost a great deal, he seemed to match the car. Only the faint smile and the twinkle in his eyes attested to the fact that this was his uniform, as surely as jeans and waterproof boots were theirs.

'How goes your Friday?' he asked.

'We're on a mission.' Tessa put her arm around him, and Eric made eye contact with Claire as if he might see some truth there. 'We're going to get Winston at the driving range to quit claiming he owns the public road.'

'Is that so?' He glanced at Claire again.

'It's true. We've been organizing all day,' Claire told him. 'In fact, Tessa was just saying she understands how you can get so consumed in a case.'

'But I get consumed for money. You two do it for love, for what you believe in. That's much more important.'

'Don't you believe in Gloria Sudbury?' Claire asked.

'I believe she acted in self-defense, and that's what matters.' He stepped forward, so close that she could smell the mint on his breath, and put his finger on her neck. 'Assume my finger is a knife. That's what Gloria lived with for six fucking years.'

Claire gasped and took a breath. 'Wow. I get it,' she said.

'Lighten up, will you, Eric?' Tessa grabbed his hand.

'Sorry, Claire,' he said. 'I've been taking the heat for my defense of this case all day. It's not the first time a woman killed in self-defense when the tormentor wasn't attacking at the time, but you'd think it was from all the press we're getting. I didn't mean to go all crazy on you.'

'I must say you're convincing.' Claire rubbed her neck. 'For a moment, I swear I could feel a knife there.'

He flashed her a smile that softened his features. 'I only wish I could get that close to the jury. They need to experience what you just did.'

'This is more than a job for you, too,' she said. 'That woman is lucky to have you defending her.'

'I hope so.' He glanced at Tessa. 'Tess, where's your purse?'

'My purse?' She shot Claire a frantic look.

'You had it earlier,' Claire said. 'The last time I saw it was on the chair in my office before we closed the greenhouses.'

'You're right. It has my notebook in it, my credit cards. I'll be right back.' She ran up the path.

'The keys,' Claire shouted and tossed them to her.

'Thanks.'

That left her and Eric. 'Let's get in the car,' he said. 'It's freezing out here.'

'I'm used to it.'

'Well, I'm not.' He opened the passenger door and went around to the other side. 'Come on.'

Claire got inside. For a moment, she thought about keeping the door open, but that was crazy.

'So how was your day?' Small talk, she thought. For once, maybe that was a good thing.

'We're just trying to get back to normal. Finding that bloodstained car still has everyone's nerves on edge.'

'Tessa's for sure. While we have a moment, I need to ask you something.'

She felt a twinge of dread. 'What's that?'

'Has Tessa ever mentioned to you that she has problems sleeping?'

'I don't think so,' she said.

'I'm surprised.' He gave her what appeared to be a casual glance but felt like much more.

'She hasn't said anything about it,' Claire replied.

'Has she mentioned any dreams?'

'Neither one of us remembers much about our dreams.'

'Nothing about a woman out there on the river?'

'No, nothing like that.' From her window of the car, the dark water beneath them stretched farther than Claire could see. 'I can understand dreaming about this place, though. We spend enough time here.'

'I'm not sure it's here – I get the feeling it's the part you can see from our deck at home, closer to the train tracks.' His profile in the moonlight was sharp and, when he turned and met her eyes, the movement was sudden. 'We both know how lonely Tessa is with Jake gone, how lost. I was short with you the other night when you brought it up.'

'We were all tired,' she said.

'You asked a good question and I ignored it.' He sighed. 'Sometimes she does forget things but I'm more worried about the nightmares. Sleep deprivation isn't going to help her loneliness and sense of loss about Jake right now.'

Claire wanted to say more. Yet she could still see Tessa's frightened expression, her fingers clutching the tissue when she begged Claire not to tell Eric that she had cried.

'If she says anything about it, I'll let you know.'

'Will you? It's no big deal. I just thought she might have mentioned something.'

'She hasn't,' Claire said, her voice firmer this time.

'You wouldn't be covering for her, would you?' The edge to Eric's voice was harder now, too.

'What's to cover for?' she asked.

'You tell me. You're best friends.'

'We are.'

'And she shares everything with you, right?'

'There's no way I would know how much she shares, Eric, but I think she's open with me and I'm sure she is with you.'

He took his notebook from the dashboard and tossed it in the back seat. It hit the leather with a snapping noise. 'Then we'll pick you up in an hour. Does that work?'

Just like that, the interrogation ended. He gave her the distant smile he had at the table the night she had tried to tell him Tessa had momentarily forgotten that Wally died.

Claire stared down at her clenched hands in her lap. 'An hour?' she asked. 'Sure. That's fine.'

Tessa

Her purse is right where she left it, on the chair. Leaving it behind has made her look absentminded, or worse. She knows Claire has been watching her, waiting for her to make a mistake. No, Claire wouldn't want to hurt her. She's just worried. Besides, Claire knows she can do her job. She has stood up to Rosemary on Tessa's behalf. That's why she's so watchful now. She knows Rosemary will pounce if any little thing Tessa handles goes wrong. Rosemary. Tessa will be glad when that hateful woman is gone.

Why does she hate me? Eric always tells Tessa she is the most loveable person he's ever met. He says everyone she meets is charmed by her. Everyone but Rosemary and Natalia.

The path ends and Tessa stops. She's lost. Every tree looks the same, and the distance between them seems to narrow. She glances down at the yellow tubular flowers drooping from low bushes. She should know the name of those flowers, but all she can think of is honeysuckle and she knows that isn't right. Even the river looks different here. Somehow, she must have wandered off her path to the other side of it. Her breath is so strained that she fears she will pass out. Maybe the parking lot is in the other direction. It's just stress getting the best of her. That car showing up. The gun, the blood. Her outburst at Winston. Claire's guarded behavior. Just stress, that's all. No one gets lost on this side of the river. Farther west maybe, but not here.

She'll be all right. Anyone can take a wrong turn. Nothing to worry about on this calm night. All she has to do is turn around and retrace her footsteps. A simple solution, as Eric would say. Eric. He'll be talking to Claire, asking questions, wondering what's taking her so long.

Ground fog lifts like swirls of smoke. Tessa moves faster, before it can wrap around her ankles. Ahead of her, beneath the gleam of moonlight, the girl appears. She is floating on the river. Tessa can't see her face, only her dress, the same color as the sky on a clear day. In the moonlight, the dress seems to illuminate her.

The girl's arms lift and Tessa realizes that she is holding something.

She points it at Tessa, and Tessa screams.

Branches crunch behind her. She tries to run, but then Timothy steps out from behind one of the trees and she chokes back a sob.

'What's wrong?' His voice is harsh, his eyes wide.

She glances down at his boots, his tan-colored work pants tucked into them. 'The sound of the branches. I was afraid.'

'You're all right.' He moves closer. 'What happened? Did you get lost again?'

'Again?' God, no. This can't have happened before.

'Follow me. You were heading the wrong way, west toward your neighborhood. It's easy to get turned around out here at night.' He reminds her of an English bobby with his straight posture and long, shiny black ponytail. Yet Timothy is real. She has not made him up.

'Yes,' she says. 'I got turned around.'

Now she recognizes the trail back to their offices.

Timothy turns with a solemn expression. 'You went right at the end of the path when you meant to go left,' he says.

'But I couldn't . . .' Tessa remembers. 'You're right. I did.'

'Best if you head the rest of your way by yourself.'

'Yes, of course, that's best.' Although giddy with relief, she tries to match his serious mood.

As she nears the car, the shadows behind the windshield take on the shapes of people – Eric and Claire, their heads close. Tessa forces a smile to her lips and walks to the passenger door. Claire jumps out and hugs her. Tessa looks into her eyes, asking without words if she has said anything to Eric about the girl, about the crying, about anything.

'We're cool,' Claire whispers.

Tessa sighs. 'Good.'

'See you in a few minutes.'

That's right. They're going to a party, picking up Claire at her house. Tessa is glad she'll have a chance to redeem herself. Eric is always proud of her when they go out in public. He likes the way she can talk to strangers, the way she can be what he calls spontaneous. That's a good goal for tonight. Spontaneous. Still, Tessa is ashamed that she forgot her purse with credit cards and, most of all, her notebook inside. He used to think nothing of that kind of behavior. Now he's always watching.

Claire heads to her car and Tessa smiles at Eric.

He smiles back and starts toward town.

'I'm so sorry.'

He seems more focused on the dirt road than her, though. 'We'll be all right,' he says. 'Bobby's parties never start on time.'

'I mean, it was so silly of me to leave my purse inside.'

'Right.'

It's almost as if she is speaking to a radio that knows what to broadcast back to her.

'Eric?' she asks.

'What?' All of a sudden he is pure focus, pure interest, his eyes on every inch of her. 'What is it, Tess?'

'I'm sorry,' she says. 'That's all.'

She feels a little better. As they drive away, Tessa sneaks a look back where they have been. No girl. No one at all. The river is full of stars.

At the River
November

The river is the sensible destination, and this entire meeting is about maintaining one's focus amid chaos. No reason to drive all over the outskirts of town when they can settle it right here. They drive in silence and she thinks about a poem, 'The Love Song of J. Alfred Prufrock,' about a man who is unable to make a decision and loses his chance at love.

She is not losing her chance. The two of them remain silent until she pulls down the one-lane road and onto the riverbank. She lowers the window and stops the car. Twelve minutes. That is as much time as she needs. Yet this is not as flawless as that poem, not as uncomplicated as the sweet air outside.

'You have a right to know what I am going to do,' she tells her passenger.

'And what is that?'

She detects defiance, a set to the jaw.

'When I leave here tonight, I am going to disappear.'

'Where are you going?'

'That doesn't matter.' Her throat is dry. She needs to get this over with, to keep her voice as strong and certain as she feels. 'When I return, things will be different.'

'Things?'

'Life,' she says. 'For me and for you, too.'

'Meaning?'

The questions anger her, so she pauses and breathes the

fresh air. Finally, she says in her best calm voice, 'Meaning that you're not in control anymore, and you need to get used to that idea right now.'

'Let me get this straight.' The laughter surprises her. 'Have you deluded yourself into thinking that you are some kind of threat to me?'

'Not at all,' she tells her passenger. 'All I'm saying is I'm leaving the past behind, and I think it's time you did the same.'

'And why is that?'

No, it is not defiance that set to the jaw. Can it be amusement?

SEVEN

Claire

Claire drove to Tessa's to pick her up for the protest along the road to the golf course early Saturday morning because Eric was *in trial mode*, as Tessa put it. As his case drew to a close, the media was probing every aspect of his client Gloria Sudbury's inconsistent history and possible infidelity with an unnamed doctor at the hospital where she worked.

Eric was fighting back, challenging reporters to examine Charles Sudbury's past as carefully as they were examining Gloria's. Charles, not his wife, had the history of abuse. Friend after friend of Gloria's testified about how he had threatened her daily with his knives, and how, near the end, he'd locked her in their bedroom when he left the house.

At the television station party the night before, Eric had spent most of his time talking to Bobby Glover, who was looking stockier than usual and wearing a Tommy Bahama sweater that matched his pale green contacts. Claire had always found Bobby charming, if too much of a crowd-pleaser. Even in conversation, he constantly glanced around the room, as if checking to see if someone more worthy of his attention had just walked in. Since his divorce, he seemed to be trying even harder to be liked, maybe even respected.

Although Eric nodded politely as Bobby continued their one-sided conversation, Claire could tell Eric was watching Tessa and her. Once, when their gazes met, the look he gave Claire was so unguarded and sad that she could tell his concerns were deeper than he had expressed to her. He seemed to be telling her that he knew more than he had shared, and Claire wondered what else was going on with Tessa.

Tessa rarely drove now and Claire didn't ask her why. She did intend to talk to her some more about the woman Tessa

thought she saw on the river. Tessa's visions, memories, whatever they were, might be grounded in reality. They needed to
follow every hunch.

That morning, they stood in Tessa's living room, what Claire
had come to think of as the public part of the house, much
more elegant than the unpretentious furniture far from the view
of those outside. Tessa seemed vibrant as she hugged Claire
in the entry hall. A long white wool scarf was draped over the
front of her puffy black vest.

'What do you think?' She gestured to the wreaths and the
massive imitation fir Christmas tree they put up every year.

'I've always loved that tree,' Claire said.

'Oh.' Tessa hesitated, looked at it again and nodded. 'That's
right. Me too. I've always loved it too.'

'Let's go. We're going to show Winston and his cronies at
the driving range that he can't keep us out,' Claire told her.
'We may even get some media coverage.'

'I don't think so.' Tessa adjusted an ornament on the tree.
'Eric told Bobby Glover to call off his dogs, meaning he didn't
want my face all over TV with this case going on and all.'

'When did he tell him that?' Claire asked. 'I did see them
in some pretty deep conversation last night.'

'Not then.' She busied herself with a silver angel and glanced
over at Claire. 'It was just this morning, on the phone.'

'You listened in?'

She nodded. 'Am I terrible?'

Eavesdropping on Eric's conversations seemed like the last
thing Tessa would do, but there was no point in bringing that
up right now. 'The Gloria Sudbury case has to be consuming
him,' Claire said. 'If you have to overhear a phone call or two
to catch up with what's going on with your husband, I'm not
going to judge you.'

'Thank you.' A smile lit her face. 'You would have judged
me for that once.'

'No, I wouldn't have.'

'Hey, you judged me once for trying to pick a flower.'

'Just trying to educate the volunteers.' She tried to joke, but
no, that wasn't right. She needed to be honest with Tessa if
she expected the same in return.

Claire thought about her mother, the only person she knew who was better educated and more distant than her father. Her mother, who liked to say, with a touch of sadness but no guilt whatsoever, that when you're raised in the desert you grow up to be a cactus.

'I admit I was more judgmental when we met,' she told Tessa. 'That was my family – right or wrong, black or white, no gray.'

'I like you better this way.' Tessa ran her fingers through the fringe of her scarf.

'Me too,' she said. 'And I'm not about to judge you now.'

'You just needed to learn how to have fun,' Tessa said. 'And we're going to have some today. Let's go.'

She opened the front door and they stepped outside into the chilly, sunlit morning.

'I wanted to tell you this at Bobby's party but didn't have a chance,' Claire said as they walked.

'Bobby!' Tessa made a face. 'It was a bit over the top, don't you think, with the station's letters on the champagne flutes and the caterers speaking French?'

'Not to mention the ratio of at least two women for every man.'

'That's Bobby,' Tessa said. 'Eric hates doing divorces, but every time he raises his fees he gets more high-priced clients, just like that guy.'

Claire paused at the car. 'I wanted to tell you a little bit about what Eric asked me when you went back for your purse last night.'

Tessa seemed to stiffen, and then she knotted the scarf around her neck. 'So that's why your heads were so close together in the car.'

Claire didn't recall her head being close to Eric's.

'He was worried that you haven't been sleeping well.'

'Sometimes I don't. And sometimes he doesn't.' She started to head for the passenger side and stopped. 'Is that all?'

Claire shook her head. 'He said you told him about seeing someone on the river.'

'I was afraid of that.' Tessa's voice broke. She glanced back at her house, her front door, as if gauging how quickly she could return there. 'You didn't tell him anything, did you?'

'I promised you I wouldn't.'

'How could he know?' she asked, as if Claire had the answer. 'Did I tell him and forget?'

'You're both under a lot of stress. It's possible you did forget. And if you don't want to go to the protest today, that's all right, too.'

'No. I do want to go.' Tessa reached for the door. 'I have to.'

'If you're sure.'

'You said you wouldn't judge me.' She stood, clutching the handle.

'I'm just concerned, not judging.' Claire forced a laugh. 'Tessa, if I can confess to you about Al, about rolling around with him on that pathetic sofa in his office, you don't have to be ashamed to tell me about something you may or may not have seen.'

'You have a point.' She giggled and got inside. 'Please tell me you're over that guy.'

Claire ignored her comment and got in, too. 'So you're sure you still want to go to the protest?'

'Absolutely. We are the protest!'

'On the way, maybe you can tell me more about what you've seen.'

Tessa leaned back against the headrest. 'I'll try. I'm just not sure if I believe myself.'

'Then we'll take what you think you saw and we'll approach it as scientists. We'll prove it true or false. How does that sound?'

Claire started the car but had no intention of moving it just yet. She wanted to share with Tessa what she had been considering. 'Think about this. What if you really did see some woman out there on the river, and what if that has something to do with the car and the bloodstains, something that would help the sheriff? Wouldn't you want to help?'

'I know where you're going with this.' Tessa half-turned in the seat. 'But Claire, what if what I saw proves that Al did have something to do with that gun and that car seat? Would you still want to hear it?'

Even as she felt the flush spread across her face, Claire knew the answer. 'Yes. Either way, I need to know what you saw.'

The drive to the river was one of the prettiest in their town, sprinkled with more trees and fewer people than anywhere else. The farther down they drove, a calming feeling made Claire want to put up the windows, regardless of the weather. This was no time to think about the view or even their protest, Claire thought. Maybe she should drive the long way, north of Tessa's house, where they could park and walk the rest. Instead, she took the easy drive, the way they would go to work, but she pulled over onto the lookout before they got on the path to the golf course. Although it was rumored that drug dealers from other locations came out here northwest of town to buy and sell, no other vehicle occupied the small space. The early morning sun was making diamond-bright sparks in the water, and the air held the promise of rain.

'It's pretty crazy,' Tessa said, and sighed. 'And I'm not going to lie about this to you. It's pretty scary.'

'Scary how?'

'Because, as I told you before, I'm not sure if she's real or not. Other things, too.'

'Like what?'

'I can't.' She squeezed her eyes shut.

Claire gestured toward the river and tried her best to sound conversational. 'Have you ever seen her here?'

Tessa nodded and rubbed her hands over the scarf as if warming her arms. 'I did a couple of times, or I thought I did.'

'Can you tell me what she looks like?'

'No, but if she showed up right now, I would recognize her. The dress is what I see most of all. Ice blue.'

'Mostly ice or mostly blue?'

'I don't know. Mostly blue, I guess, but I don't know. Glacial. Is that a word?'

'I'm trying to picture it,' Claire said. 'What makes you think she might not be real?'

'Because she shows up when no one else is around.' Tessa shivered. 'And last night, when I went back for my purse, I saw her again.'

'So that's why you were so distracted,' Claire said.

'Worse than distracted. She pointed something at me and I thought she had a gun.'

'You've got to tell someone.'

'Tell them what?'

'You've got to tell Eric – the gun part, at least.'

'I can't.'

'But he's worried,' Claire said.

'He's also risking everything on this Sudbury case. He doesn't have time for a crazy wife right now.'

'You're not crazy.' She squeezed Tessa's arm and forced her to make eye contact. 'Whatever you saw was important, even though we don't know what it means yet. Maybe it's connected to the car Timothy found. Maybe it's connected to something else. But it's important, and all you have to do is remember as much as you can.'

'Thank you for believing me.' Except for her trembling lip, Tessa's smile stayed the same.

'I'll always believe you.'

'Will you?' Her voice trailed off.

'Yes.'

'And if Eric asks you about me again, you'll tell him I'm fine? That there's nothing wrong with me?'

Claire tried to decide whether or not she could keep that promise, and finally said, 'I won't tell him anything you don't want me to.'

Tessa

Tessa is good at leading, and none of their volunteers at the protest would even imagine the conversation she and Claire had just shared in the car. They chanted, carried signs and disrupted the golf course's happy little clubhouse. That was the goal: draw attention to their cause. The few members sitting in the clubhouse got up and left. Not that anyone would play in this weather, but their departure from the building, their unfinished meals visible through the window, showed how little support Winston had.

Now that she's home, with no one to lead, with only silence

in the house, Tessa feels uneasy again. The Christmas tree in the living room seems to mock her. From the moment Claire came in the house and admired it this morning – saying she'd always liked it – she had looked at Tessa in a strange way, as if she had caught her doing something wrong again, as if Tessa had forgotten it or something. She would not forget the family tree, could never forget the faces of Jake and Eric on Christmas Eve, but that was at the other place, before she and Eric found this house on the San Joaquin River Bluffs.

She's not sure why she's thinking of her mother's pancakes all of a sudden. Maybe it's because of the awful food they had at the party last night. Now, though, her kitchen smells like the lentil curry she hurried to get on the stove earlier when Eric said he would actually be home for dinner. Late, though. He's always late these days, but it will be over soon and his client will be free. They always are. In spite of the curry, her mother's pancakes are what fill her senses as she stands at the sink, washing the cutting board, the measuring cup, the paring knife with its burgundy handle.

Washing the dishes by hand uses less water. Besides, Tessa likes the way her mind drifts and her hands move separately, needing no direction. Suds. Rinse. Place on the slanted wood draining board. It's that simple, that soothing. As the water leaves the sink in slow swirls, she remembers the sharp, sweet smell of powdered sugar her mother sifted over the top of each pancake. She wasn't a perfect mother, but when Tessa thinks about her, the thought of pancakes overshadows everything else.

The dishes washed, Tessa tells herself she can use this time alone to work on the campaign for the protest, although now it seems almost frivolous. She tiptoes to the balcony and then has to laugh at herself. This is her house. She can look out of her own window if she wants to.

The river stretches out calm and quiet, as if it has given up all it has to offer. If there is a girl, if she really saw a girl, let her be there. And let her be all right. She wants to save this girl the way she and Claire want to save the river, the way Eric wants to save Gloria.

I can save her, Tessa thinks. *I just need some help.*

Tessa cracks open the door and steps out. This might a good night for a walk. Fresh air. A chance to think and, yes, a chance to look for the woman in the ice-blue dress. But what if Eric comes back and finds her gone? Better to drive. That way, if he gets home before she does, she can tell him that she was at the store, not walking after dark. He wouldn't want her doing that.

She parks her car along the cul-de-sac beside the sloping sidewalk that leads down to the river. No one will be out here this late. Any activity would take place on the east side where their office and the golf course are. But this is the part of the river she watches from her kitchen window and balcony. This is where the city ends. There's nothing after it except the river below.

Tessa gets out of the car and looks up at the back of her house. She has left the outside lights on. They illuminate the teak patio furniture and the chaise where Eric likes to relax with a drink. She can almost see him in the doorway, stepping outside, and herself, coming up behind him, leaning down and rubbing his shoulders. Funny how she can watch Eric and her while she's standing here looking up at them.

Tessa walks down the sidewalk, just partway. The path is too rough and, even with the pepper spray in her handbag, the place feels too desolate. Yet she is drawn to the sense of peace here tonight: the silence of the stars, the vastness of the sky.

Either the girl is really here or she is some kind of hallucination. Tessa needs to figure out which. At the end of the sidewalk, the dirt path heads in two directions – left toward the bridge where the train tracks cross the river on their way northwest, and right, down closer to the water. Tessa stands between the two and looks straight ahead where, maybe one hundred feet or so away, the river flows.

For a moment, she thinks the girl is standing on the other side, but only the shapes of bushes huddle along the water's edge.

A cold breeze tickles her neck.

'Are you out there?' she asks, and feels silly.

'I'm over here. Don't be afraid.'

It is a man's voice.

Tessa gasps and almost chokes on her own breath.

'Don't be afraid,' he says again, and walks slowly up the path on her right.

'Timothy!' Tessa tries to control her breathing and her voice, which has shot high.

'I didn't mean to scare you, ma'am.'

'What are you doing out here?'

'Just checking the area like I always do after everyone goes home. What about you?'

For the first time, Tessa realizes how tall he is – taller than Claire, taller than Eric, even. She starts to put her hand in her bag, just to touch the container of pepper spray, but that's silly. Timothy is her friend. He just took her by surprise, that's all.

'I felt like taking a walk,' she tells him.

'Why now?' Timothy's eyes seem to widen in the moonlight.

She knows he's wondering if she's lost, like she was the night of Bobby Glover's party.

'I live right up there.' She points at her house, which seems miles away. 'I know where I am.'

'It's changed now,' he says, and glances out toward the river. 'Not just because of the protest today over at the golf course. Not even because of the car we found. Too many people wandering around out here, especially at night.'

'I haven't seen anyone down here.'

'It's just a matter of time. Your husband will worry.'

'He's fine,' Tessa replies too quickly.

'You sure?' He crosses his arms in an awkward interrogation stance.

He's not home. That's what she wants to tell him, but she is afraid to in case Timothy is not what he appears. Instead, she says, 'Seeing that mangled car seat and the gun upset me. I guess that's why I'm here.'

He nods as if acknowledging the truth. 'But it's not safe for you, a lady alone this late at night.'

'It's barely seven o'clock.'

'What about the homeless people? See that cart over there?' He nods toward an abandoned Whole Foods cart missing a wheel and shoved up against the fence outside the path leading down under the train tracks.

'It's been there all year,' she says. 'I can see it from my patio.'

'Like I said, it's different now.' He glances around, as if trying to measure distances and danger. 'Just because you don't see them don't mean they aren't here.'

The knowing grin he gives her makes Tessa wonder if he is talking about homeless people or someone else. If the girl is out here, and Timothy has seen her too, that would be proof she could take to Eric.

'Tell me about them,' she says.

'Maybe another time.' He takes a step toward her. 'Did you bring your own vehicle or can I give you a ride home?'

She stares down at his foot in its mud-crusted boot. 'I don't need a ride, thanks. And I want to look around before I leave.'

'It's not safe for you.' Timothy clenches his teeth as if to hold back something that has been building up in him. 'I maybe shouldn't say this, but that car we found . . . It was tore up.'

'Maybe it was in the water a long time.'

'No, ma'am,' he says. 'I broke up my own cars and trucks when I was younger and working for Pick-A-Part, and I can tell you it's not easy. No human could do what we found out there.'

She gazes past him to a shape on the ground and starts toward it.

Her eyes adjust to the dim light, and she focuses on a small, formless bag that someone might take to the gym.

'What's that?'

'Just my tools.' Timothy moves closer to her. 'Tessa . . . ma'am, I don't mean any disrespect, but you need to leave now.'

She starts to tell him that she can be anywhere she wants to be in her own neighborhood but doesn't want to argue. 'What kind of tools?' she asks.

'River tools.'

But the bag looks soft. Again, she thinks of gym clothes and wonders if Timothy is too shy to admit he works out.

'I'll leave in a minute, but I want to ask you something first. May I do that, Timothy?'

He cocks his head, and she can tell he likes the question and its implications of deference on her part.

'I guess so, as long as you ask it while I walk you back the way you came.'

'Over there.' Without moving, she gestures toward the water. 'Do you ever see her?'

He glances down at his feet and then back at her. 'Let's get you to your car.'

'No.' Her voice comes out too sharp. 'I mean, please tell me, Timothy. You're out here because you are looking for something too.'

'Maybe.'

'You know what I'm talking about, don't you? Have you ever seen her?'

He glances back at the very spot Tessa suspected the girl would be. 'Not tonight.'

Finally, a witness. 'But before? You did, didn't you?'

'Ma'am,' he says. 'I told you that you shouldn't be out here, and I know your husband leaves his phone number with us in case your friend Doctor Barrett is unavailable and you need him to pick you up.'

'What about it?' Tessa tries to swallow but her throat feels like sandpaper.

'All I mean is that if you're having a problem driving or anything, I could call him for you.'

'That's hardly necessary.' She glares at him. 'I can drive, for heaven's sake.'

'As I said then, I'll walk you up the path to your car.'

Tessa allows him to do so because as much as she wants him to tell her more about seeing the girl, she can't risk Eric worrying about her right now. The smell of eucalyptus blows in along with the cooling breeze. For a moment, Timothy frightened her, but not now.

Tessa looks up at him. 'Why do you care what happens to me?'

'Because.' He seems to think about it. 'Because Wally would want me to.'

'Wally's dead.'

'That doesn't change what he'd want me to do.'

She is pleased that she remembered about Wally this time. But there's something else that she remembers, and it makes her uncomfortable with every step to the car. A bulky gym bag. A bag that doesn't belong out here.

EIGHT

Claire

J ake would be coming home from college for the holidays, but Claire didn't note much difference in Tessa. On Saturday, she had acted as if she didn't even recognize her own Christmas tree. Yet once they were actually protesting at Winston's driving range, Tessa had taken charge and directed the others with the same ease she displayed in her classroom visits.

Claire knew what her mother would say had she asked for advice. Her father wouldn't say anything – not when he could write another article for an esoteric science journal instead of communicating with the family.

'Find the cause,' her mother would tell Claire. 'Research the history.'

Other than talking about being raised by her father and describing her mother's beauty and cooking skills, Tessa hadn't shared much about her family, and Claire wasn't about to pry now. Instead, she wanted to convince Tessa to talk to Eric about that girl she thought she saw in the river. Eric was smart and he loved his wife. Claire couldn't help thinking that she was making a mistake by not insisting Tessa tell him what she had seen.

Then she reminded herself that she was not the woman she had once been, the woman who didn't know how to reach out and be a friend to anyone, the woman who was only comfortable when speaking about science. She had changed, and she knew she was doing the right thing to keep what Tessa had told her to herself, at least for now.

That night, they went out for their annual holiday dinner, minus Danny, of course. At Tessa's insistence, they had dressed up – Eric in a dark suit, Tessa in burgundy and Claire in a green velvet dress Danny had bought for her a few years ago.

So, in a way, Danny was here anyway, she thought as they

sat in a circular booth of Arroyo West, a seafood restaurant
in which Bobby Glover had purchased an interest. Bobby was
working the room that night, complete with a white fluffy
chef's toque on his head, even though he didn't go near the
kitchen. Bobby Junior was waiting tables. The mingled smells
of fish and garlic filled the glassed-in patio with its heat lamp.
Sitting between Tessa and Eric in the booth, Claire tried to
relax.

Speaking about the Sudbury case, Eric told them he
was certain he could prove Gloria Sudbury's husband had
terrorized her.

'It's not a murder case,' he said. 'It's self-defense. Spousal
abuse.'

When he spoke like this, when it was only the three of them,
he possessed a magic Claire had never witnessed in anyone
– not Danny, not even Al. It wasn't the high-drama mode he
displayed in the courtroom. When Eric spoke intimately and
honestly, his voice low, he became the most passionate, decent
man Claire had ever known.

Tessa hugged him. 'I love you,' she told him, 'but I have
to pee.'

When Tessa went to the bathroom, Eric nudged Claire. 'OK,
you can come clean with me,' he said. 'What's bothering you?'

'I'm fine,' she lied. 'Just tired.'

'And stressed, I'll bet. Have you been able to talk to Liz?'

'Not yet. She asked for space and I'm respecting that.'

'Danny's behind it, that bastard.' He patted her hand. 'Jake
will be arriving in a couple of days. You need to come over.'

'I will. I miss him.'

'Me too.' He picked up the menu and put it down again.
'So much has changed since the last time we all went out like
this. For both of us.'

'For *all* of us,' Claire said.

As they looked at each other, his eyes misty, he said, 'I'll
never be able to thank you enough for what you've done for
Tess.'

'She's my friend, Eric.'

'You know what I mean.' He squeezed her hand on the
table.

'What's going on here?' Tessa approached them and looked down at their hands.

'Just telling Claire how much we appreciate her,' Eric said.

Tessa slid into the seat beside him. 'Move over,' she told him.

'Everything OK?' he asked.

'Sure,' she said. 'Let's start with chowder, just like always.'

For a moment, Claire felt guilty, but she had no reason to. Her momentary closeness to Eric hadn't brought on the guilt; Tessa's expression had. The evening went downhill from there. Tessa complained that there was too much tabasco in the chowder, too much cheese in the garlic bread. She picked at the scampi, said it was no better than what she cooked at home, ate one, maybe two shrimp and seemed generally distracted. Before the meal was over, she knocked over her water glass.

'You need to tell me what's wrong,' Claire said the next morning after they'd left their office and headed out along the bluffs.

'I just have a lot on my mind.'

They stopped and looked out over the gray water.

'You weren't upset with Eric and me?'

'Why should I be?'

'You shouldn't. I just wanted to be sure.'

'I wasn't accusing you of hitting on my husband, if that's what you mean.' Tessa's smile looked forced.

'What then?' Claire asked.

Tessa stopped on the path. 'When I went to the bathroom, I got lost on the patio.'

'That's easy to do,' Claire said. The place was a labyrinth. 'I would have gotten lost too. We probably should have gone together.'

'And then when I found my way back and saw you and Eric holding hands . . .'

'We weren't holding hands, Tessa,' she said.

'That's how it looked.'

'We were talking about you,' Claire told her. 'I realize everything's changed with Danny out of the picture, but you have got to know you can trust me.'

'Sometimes I don't trust anyone.'

'Well, you have to trust me,' Claire said. 'You and Eric and I are just the way we've always been. I would never betray you. I've never told him anything you've shared with me.'

'I realize that most of the time.' Tessa shook her head. 'I don't know what's wrong with me anymore.'

She glanced down below them. 'What's that?' She pointed at an island, one of many little ones on the river. This one was farther away, though, like a piece of land drifting slowly south. Covered with dark green scrub, it looked smaller than the others only because of its location.

Claire tried to see what Tessa was pointing out. Something white and round bobbed up next to the island.

'Vegetation,' she told Tessa. But the blob grew bigger, more bloated. 'Maybe an animal.'

Claire squinted and moved closer to the edge of the bluff. The shape, whatever it was, flopped in the water, its backside pointing up. 'Oh my God,' Claire whispered. It was human, or it had been once.

'It's a person.' Tessa grabbed Claire's arm. 'It's a person, isn't it?' Claire tried to calm Tessa. She tried to calm herself.

'Come on,' she said, fighting nausea. 'Let's get in the car. I've got to call the sheriff.'

Tessa began to sob.

'Hang on,' Claire told her, but she was shaking so violently that she could barely hold her phone. 'It's going to be all right. We'll call the sheriff, and then we'll call Eric.'

Tessa stopped crying, but she continued to stare at the body in the river. This was no accident, Claire knew. This was no drowning victim. This was the moment she had both feared and wanted from the time Timothy pulled the car out of the river.

Tessa

Jake sits at the kitchen table overlooking the patio, and watching him makes Tessa feel tense. Her fingers around the handles of the warm glass baking dish tremble. Eric thinks she is OK now that Jake is back on holiday break. He says he can see how relaxed she is, how happy, but she doesn't feel any different than she did before. Not that she isn't glad to have him here, but all of that joy cannot erase what she's seen. She tried to believe that bloated shape bobbing in the water was anything else until, right before her, the thing became a body and she could no longer lie to herself.

Jake glances up from the table, his eyes crystal blue like Eric's, lashes so thick they appear to be outlined. He has her hair, though, full, black and stubborn. Running his fingers through it, he picks up his fork and says, 'Thanks, Mom. I'm starving.'

She has prepared macaroni and cheese, comfort food from his childhood. Many nights during those early years when Eric had left the big law firm and was going out on his own, she was the only one here to sit down to dinner with Jake. She cooked according to his whims then anything he ordered: mac and cheese, tuna-noodle casseroles, Chinese chicken salads, pizzas piled high with whatever outlandish combination he desired.

'Why are you so quiet?' Jake asks.

'Just thinking of all those crazy pizzas we used to make. French fries and hummus. Ugh.'

'You spoiled me rotten,' he says. 'You still do.'

'I must have done all right,' she tells him. 'You didn't turn out so badly.'

When he finishes the meal, he pushes his tall, rangy frame from the table and says, 'Perfect. Mind if I head over to Bobby's now?'

'What about the brownies?'

'I thought I'd take a couple with me.'

She picks up his empty plate. 'Wouldn't you rather hang out here until Dad gets home?'

'I'll be back before then.'

She carries the dishes to the sink and then turns to face him. 'I don't know.'

'Why? Because Bobby got in a little trouble?'

'I'm not trying to pick your friends for you,' she says.

'You're not?' He gets out of his chair. 'What are you trying to do then?'

He's mastered Eric's use of questions to get the upper hand in an argument.

'I guess I'd just like to spend a little more time with you,' she says.

'I missed you too, Mom.' He walks over and joins her. Together at the sink, they look through the patio doors into the darkness that holds the river. 'But Bobby's a good guy. I've done things just as stupid as what he did.'

'Stolen money?' She grips the side of the sink.

'Of course not.' He shakes his head and laughs. 'Mom, lighten up. All I mean is that Bobby got caught doing something he shouldn't have done and would probably never do again.'

He hugs her and walks into the living room. Tessa follows, her hands still wet. She's not going to argue with him. Besides, he's probably right. The Glover boy has never been a bad kid.

'What do you think of the new tree?' she asks. 'Your dad got it for me.'

He stops and turns slowly. 'What are you talking about?' he asks her. 'This is the same tree we've had for years.'

'The same tree.' That's what has been bothering her. It explains Claire's comment earlier. Eric said it was new and she believed him. Or she thought it was new, and he went along with it. Something like that. 'The same tree, yes. That's right.'

He studies her face. 'You were just kidding me, weren't you?'

'I got tongue-tied,' she tells him. 'You knew what I meant, though. Say hi to Bobby for me.'

'I don't think I'll go.'

'That's silly. You want to, and as you said, you haven't seen him since you left.'

'He'll understand.' A flush spreads over his face.

'Understand what, Jake?' Tessa's voice rises. She can't control it.

'That I want to spend time with my mom.'

'You can do that later. We'll have plenty of opportunities to hang out while you're here.'

'Mom.' He reaches out for her arm and pulls her toward him. 'I know it had to be awful finding that dead woman.'

'I didn't find her.' She moves away from him. 'I just saw her.'

'It's the same thing.' He nudges her with his elbow. 'Come on. Let's have a brownie together. I'd like another cup of that great coffee of yours.'

But Tessa no longer wants him to stay. It's as if he's afraid to leave her alone, as if what she said about the tree scared him. She lets him hug her, and then she takes him by the shoulders, looking up into his eyes. 'I'm all right, Jake.'

They stare at each other for a moment, and finally he says, 'Are you sure?'

'You were right in the first place. Finding that woman was terrible. I never saw a dead person before.'

'Oh, Mom. I'm sorry.'

'And I'm sorry I worried you,' she tells him. 'Believe me, I'm not so far gone that I could forget our family Christmas tree.'

'I know that.' He doesn't bother to hide his sigh of relief.

She nods toward the front door. 'You go see your friend. Dad and I will be here when you get back.'

He hugs her again and gives her a grin that reminds her of Eric. Tessa stands at the door and watches him walk the circular drive to the car, get in and finally leave. At least she has the Christmas tree straight in her mind now. But no wonder she got confused. All she can think about now is the body in the river.

'Are you there?' she whispers the way she did on the bluffs the night Timothy stepped out with the satchel and scared her.

No one answers. Good. At least she hasn't seen the girl.

Tessa's cheeks burn with the cold. 'Frostbite,' she says and remembers another time. Frostbite, she thinks. She could have lost her fingers.

Tessa blows on them and knows she is safe, not locked out of her mother's house the way she was that other time.

Headlights spill onto the driveway. Eric's car. How long has she been standing here? She closes the door and runs to the kitchen. The clock begins to chime. That's impossible. It can't be ten. The balcony blinds are still open. Tessa goes over to close them as she hears Eric closing the garage door.

On the other side of the river, she sees a blur of light in the fog. She moves closer to the blinds. A figure comes into focus, not her face, but the outline of her, standing there in an ice-blue dress.

NINE

Claire

With the discovery of the body at the river, the place Claire once loved now unnerved her. How much else, she wondered, had gone on out here? How much still was? As much as she wanted answers, she also feared them. No one was talking but Claire knew it would only be a matter of time before whatever happened would be revealed.

The sheriff's department officers arrived and spoke to everyone, including Claire. The deputy who interviewed her, an older, softly spoken man who reminded her of Wally, told her that the body she and Tessa had found was female.

'Have you identified her?' Claire asked.

'Not yet, ma'am.'

He didn't say why not, but she knew what happened to fingerprints when a body had been in the water too long. DNA and dental records required a public record of some kind, and the part of the car Timothy had found didn't have a vehicle identification number, so they hadn't been able trace it. The department would begin investigating missing persons reports for possible matches and they would begin dragging the area again, trying to find the rest of the car.

Unlike some men, the deputy didn't seem bothered by the fact that she was taller than he was. As he sat at the counter by the front window, he motioned outside. 'You have a pretty good view here.'

'My office is in the back,' she said, and pointed at the partition hiding her cubbyhole. 'But we're coming and going all day through the front.'

'Have you noticed any strangers in the area?' he asked.

She thought about the deputy's question and said, 'In a way, we have strangers out here all the time. That's the point of holding tours and classes.'

'Anyone who stood out, who stuck in your mind for some reason?'

'There are some homeless people,' she said. 'Since the city destroyed their camps downtown, a few of them have come out here.'

'Can you describe them?'

'They stay out of sight, and there aren't that many of them.'

He pulled out his chair and walked over to the window. 'Who lives in that white camper out there?'

'No one.' She got up and joined him. 'We store supplies there.'

He wrote something in his notebook. 'Any new employees in, say, the last year?'

'You'd need to check with Rosemary, our director, for that. We have interns during the summer but she could tell you more about them.'

'I've already talked to Ms Boudreaux.' He turned from the view. 'Tell me about the gun.'

'It was there in the car,' Claire stammered. 'We all saw it.'

'Can you describe it?'

This was a test, she knew. Of course he was aware of what kind of gun it was. The sheriff's department had taken possession of it.

'A German Luger,' she said.

'Do you know anyone with a gun like that?'

'No.' It wasn't a lie. Al didn't have his anymore. 'No one relevant.'

'Allan Paden isn't relevant?'

'No,' Claire said. 'He's not.'

He wrote something else in his book. Then he gave her his card, told her to contact him if she remembered anything and said he might want to speak to her again. By the time he left, Claire was trembling.

Rosemary walked through the office on her way outside, and Claire waited for the snide comment she was sure would come.

'I'll be back later this afternoon,' Rosemary said.

She was probably the one who had told the deputy about Al's gun, but she was taking no obvious pleasure from her action. The horror of the situation must have gotten to her, too. Rosemary was as shocked as the rest of them.

Over the holiday break, they began moving her office and the rest of the river conservancy to the university science building and greenhouse complex. The river office up from the golf course was tense with the sheriff's deputies still methodically dragging the area, looking for evidence. Their presence made it difficult to continue with any of the usual on-site education programs, and Claire could see the strain it put on Tessa to give presentations in the same area where they had seen the woman's body and where investigations were underway.

Although the relocation had long been part of the plan, because of the increasing presence of law enforcement, Rosemary and the board decided to expedite the process and move them to the university's greenhouse complex the Saturday after Christmas.

Claire's mother would approve. She had said, as consolation for Claire going to work in this Central California agricultural community of Fresno and not at Stanford or UC Berkeley, 'Well, at least it's a college town, and college towns have more firepower.' *Firepower*. It wasn't the kind of word Claire's mother used, and it was probably something Claire's sweet brother Hank had said to justify her career, which was modest compared to those of his and their parents.

The greenhouse complex, which covered more than one acre, included four greenhouses of living collections and dryland, tropical and carnivorous species, along with orchids, a pond and an area of plants native to the Central Valley and the surrounding foothills of the Sierra Nevada range. Timothy offered to move the snakes, Colby and Roscoe, and Tessa insisted on accompanying him in his truck. As acting restoration technician, he could decide whether or not the job fell within his duties, but Timothy had been trained by Wally and, like him, did whatever he could to help the river conservancy team.

Claire drove behind them, watching Tessa's impatient gestures as she sat sideways next to Timothy's stoic form. She spoke with such passion, such familiarity, that Claire felt as if she should look away. Once they were alone, maybe Tessa would explain how she came to know Timothy so well, or maybe Claire could just ask. She and Tessa told each other everything, or they used to.

In the small back university lot, Timothy pulled into a parking place and got out of his truck as Tessa continued her tirade. Claire parked as well, got out and lifted a box of office supplies from the back seat. The smell of greenery drifted out and already she felt calmer.

'I'll take those,' Timothy said. 'Tessa has your snakes.'

'Her snakes, maybe. Not mine.'

Claire's attempt at humor failed to diffuse the tension. Tessa bit her lip.

Wearing what looked like a new khaki shirt and pants, Timothy moved in front of them like a ranger stepping onto a trail that only he could navigate. They followed him down the pebbled path that was protected from public view by a greenhouse on each side. The cool air smelled of wet leaves, and the feeling of peace that settled over Claire convinced her that this was the right move for all of them.

Timothy gestured to a door on her right. 'Here we are.'

He pulled it open and Claire stepped into a lab room with sinks and long tables flanked by occasional stools. At the end of one table, a microscope and a Dark Star coleus plant sat side by side. Probably the usual light-against-the-leaf experiment for students, Claire guessed. Even in the dim room, the green-trimmed, velvety purple leaves were vibrant.

On the wall by the sink above a grouping of other, smaller species, someone had tacked a sign: *Beware. Carnivorous plants.*

'It's the Little Shop of Horrors, only it's not little at all,' Claire said. 'This place is huge.'

Tessa ignored her and whispered something to Timothy. As flighty as she could appear sometimes, and as much as Claire worried about her memory lapses, Tessa was never rude like this.

To the left, an open door led to two rectangular offices separated by a sliding glass door. Each had a toilet and a refrigerator which, although old and institutional, still gave the place the feeling of isolation and privacy. After the openness and lack of privacy at the river office, this was perfect.

'Which one do you want?' Claire asked Tessa.

'Doesn't matter.'

Claire moved closer to one of the tables that held a plant covered in small dark knobs. 'Oh, look, Tessa,' she said, and gestured toward one of them. 'These are coffee beans.'

Standing just inside the door and holding the snake cage, she glared at Timothy. 'Tell her.'

'Tell me what?' Claire asked. 'Tessa, put down that cage, will you?'

'She won't believe me.' Timothy placed the cardboard box on the table beside the coleus. 'They never do.'

'You have to take a chance.' Tessa's voice echoed in the large room. 'This is too important.'

'Stop.' Tessa clutched the cage as if she were ready to toss it. 'We're not going anywhere until you tell her what you told me.'

'Why don't you do as she asks, Timothy?' Claire said.

'I can't.'

Tessa slapped the coffee plant and sent it sailing.

Claire leaned down to pick up the plant and tried to think how to comfort her. 'What's going on, Timothy?' she asked in as calm a voice as she could muster.

He shook his head.

'What is it, Tessa?' She placed the plant back on the table.

'Ask him.'

Timothy glanced at a coffee bean that had rolled next to the metal wastebasket. 'Sorry, ma'am.'

'If you have something to tell me, just do it, and then let's get back to work. We have a lot of boxes here and not much time.'

He looked down at his boots. 'No one ever believes me,' he said. 'Rosemary, for example. She raises her voice when she talks to me, like she thinks I'm deaf.'

'Rosemary isn't here,' Claire said. 'I am, and I know you're an honest person.'

'I can't,' he said. 'I don't want no trouble.'

'Nobody will hurt you,' Claire said.

'You sure about that?'

'Yes. Absolutely. We think the world of you, Timothy. Wally used to say he could set his watch by you. Remember?'

He smiled, and Tessa seemed to relax, too. Claire could feel her own breathing quicken, though.

'Tell her,' Tessa said. 'He saw her, Claire. Timothy saw the girl on the river.'

'Is that true?' Claire asked.

'Yes, ma'am. I seen her. A girl in a blue dress. It was late at night and she was on the other side there.' He pointed as if they were standing on the bank. 'It was raining, and she had something tied around her head, a scarf kind of thing.'

Still clutching the snake cage, Tessa flashed her a smile. 'Tell her the rest, Timothy.'

'She was crying,' he said. 'And she was with someone. A man.'

Tessa

Timothy goes outside to bring in more boxes and Tessa arranges the snake cage in a dim corner so Roscoe and Colby can get used to their new surroundings. Before she leaves, she will place them in the area that mimics their natural habitat of rice fields and drainage canals.

This new office is spread out, not crammed in the way they were on the river. Their coffee mugs – Claire's shaped like a glass laboratory beaker, and Tessa's, a retro sea-green cup Eric bought for her on one of their trips to the coast – sit on the counter beside the microwave.

Tessa unpacks a box of books and begins arranging them on the metal shelf. As she divides them into two rows, one for students and one for donors, something causes her to look up. Claire has approached soundlessly from behind and now stands on the other side of the open cardboard box without glancing at the books inside.

'Would you like some tea?' Claire asks and places two silk packets of Mighty Leaf on the desk.

'I'm fine.'

'Water?'

Tessa does feel parched. Her lips are cracked and, when she runs her tongue over them, they taste bitter. Then she remembers how she raised her voice at poor Timothy.

'I can get it. And I'm sorry about all that.' She waves toward the next room.

Claire walks to the water cooler by the doorway. It gurgles as she fills their mugs. 'I'm glad you're OK.' She hands the cup to Tessa.

'Timothy is afraid to speak up for himself. I had to insist.'

'When did he tell you that he had seen the same woman you did?'

'He mentioned it on the way over.' She hates lying to Claire, but her head hurts and she needs to stop the questions.

'Have you seen her again?'

Tessa tries to remember, but all she sees when she closes her eyes is a blur of blue. 'I'm not sure,' she says as she perches on the edge of the desk.

Claire nods, obviously unsatisfied with her answer. 'Not since that night with the gun?'

'I'm not sure it was a gun.' She looks down at the empty cup and wishes she had more water. 'You won't tell Eric about what happened, will you?'

'Don't you want him to know that Timothy saw the woman too?'

'It doesn't matter.'

'To him or to you?'

Tessa walks to the water cooler. 'I don't know.' All of a sudden, she is tired of thinking about it. Claire stays put but Tessa knows she is watching her. Claire in her pressed white shirt and khaki pants, with her questions as casual as her messy braid.

'Why don't you go home early?' Claire says. 'We both tried to do too much today.'

'I'm fine.' Tessa isn't sure why, but she doesn't want to be alone in the car with Claire. She would like to go home, though, to lie on her clean, cool sheets, close her eyes and just think.

'Well, let me know if you change your mind.' Claire looks at her own cup as if wanting to fill it up but Tessa can see that it is still full. 'When you saw that girl . . .' Claire begins.

'Yes?' Her voice is sharper than she intends but Claire doesn't seem to notice.

'Was there a man with her the way Timothy said?'

'Yes.' She hopes that is enough but Claire continues studying her.

'What did this man look like?'

'I don't know, Claire. It was dark.'

'Even so, you must remember something. Can't you describe him?'

'He wasn't tall.' The words drift from her lips. 'Not short, kind of average, I guess, but definitely not tall. His hair was brown, probably.'

'But you couldn't see his face?'

Tessa starts to say no, but then she has to catch her breath and takes a long drink from her cup. 'Glasses,' she says. 'That's right. The man was wearing glasses.'

TEN

Claire

Lots of men wore glasses. Any number of them could have met Tessa's description of the man on the river, assuming, of course, she had seen anyone at all. Yet every time Claire thought about the man Tessa had described, she saw Al.

He was on her mind more than usual, and she hesitated before hanging the photo of a sunset he had taken for her. But it had been on the wall of the other office, and when Al had given it to her, it had been a gesture of friendship.

After more weeks of protests and pressure by the mayor, Winston, the golf-course owner, tried to compromise by offering his facility to the river group for one of its many fundraising pancake breakfasts. The sheriff's department had only a couple of officers searching now, and Tessa had stopped talking about the woman on the river.

To anyone who didn't know her well, Tessa was as upbeat as always, but Claire could tell when she forgot something or pretended to keep up with a conversation that had left her behind. She did it with a tilt of her head and an innocent smile. She did it by repeating the last words the other person had said. No one else seemed to notice, except perhaps Rosemary.

That Saturday, they were returning to their old location to host a pancake breakfast. Claire arrived early. The bluffs beyond the driving range overlooked the trees along the bank of the river. The branches had already thickened into a blur of green. Spring would arrive and depart early. Tessa and her volunteers would be in charge of the event, but with the way Tessa had been acting lately, Claire wanted to get there before everyone else.

She didn't, though. As she got out of her car, she spotted Rosemary leaning against the side of the clubhouse facing the path, a cobalt-blue scarf wrapped around her neck. The woman looked as if she lived on ice water – not just because of her thin frame, more as if coldness seemed to come from within.

The lifted eyebrow she directed at Claire conveyed that she had been there a while. But her impatience wouldn't get her far today. If she didn't want to be locked out, she should have realized that Claire was the only one with a key.

'Hi, Rosemary. You're here early.'

'So are you.'

'Just making sure everything is set up.'

'Isn't that Tessa's job?'

'She and her crew did most of it last night.' Claire hoped she hadn't stretched the truth as she unlocked the door and they walked inside to the relative warmth of the clubhouse. Tessa and her volunteers had polished the long counter and griddle facing the front window. Two new-looking stainless-steel coffee makers sat on one end, and on the other a pewter-colored mixer that could easily handle eight or nine quarts of batter. Everything looked in place and ready to go.

Not even Rosemary could criticize the setup. She stood there, silently taking in the immaculate room.

'It looks perfect to me,' Claire said. 'Shall I put on the coffee?'

'If you like. I want to talk to you before the others get here.'

'This is officially my day off,' Claire said as pleasantly as possible. 'We're volunteering for this, you know.'

'It's about Tessa.'

Claire picked up a measuring cup and scooped the French roast into the basket. 'She'll be here any minute. Can it wait?'

'I wouldn't be here if it could.' Rosemary pulled a stool to the other side of the counter. Claire cringed at the sound it made as Rosemary dragged it across the tile floor. 'Yesterday, she left the two snakes at a school. Forgot them.'

So that was it. The smell of coffee filled the room. Claire turned the spigot and filled her cup while the coffee was still gurgling through the grounds.

'She was in a hurry. Timothy Slates picked them up within the hour.'

'That's hardly his job.'

'He was available, so he went.' Claire pulled up a stool of her own. 'I don't have a problem with it.'

'You don't have a problem that our employee left a cage of snakes at an elementary school? What if they had gotten out?'

'Roscoe and Colby are harmless.' This argument wasn't getting them anywhere, and Claire needed to stop the conversation before Tessa arrived. 'But I did talk to her about it, and she agrees that she needs to be more careful.'

'The problem is more than carelessness.' Her lips pressed together, which brought out thin vertical lines that Claire had never noticed before. 'Tessa isn't representing us well professionally.'

'The kids love her and so do the teachers.'

'Anyone can collect a few letters of appreciation.'

Through the window, Claire saw two couples on bicycles pedal up to the bluffs. She poured the tasteless coffee down the sink. 'Tessa needs this job.'

'Eric has plenty of money.'

'That's not what I mean by "needs."' She decided to simply say what she thought. 'What do you really have against her?'

Color shot to Rosemary's cheeks. 'This isn't a personal concern.'

'You've called her a rich bitch since the day she came here as a volunteer, and you fought against our hiring her. Now you're suggesting that she isn't professional yet we've never had a single complaint about her. You and Natalia are the only people I know who don't like her.'

'Quite the contrary.' Rosemary rose from the stool. 'And quite frankly, you have no idea who Natalia does or doesn't like. It's her husband you're interested in, and you have been all along, even before they divorced.'

'That's not true, and we aren't talking about Al here,' Claire said. 'We're talking about your efforts to sabotage one of our best employees, an employee who doesn't deserve it. I spoke to the teacher myself. She was fine with what happened, and they have the highest regard for Tessa.'

'I'm not talking about the teacher.' In the light from the

window, her face took on a yellowish cast. 'I'm talking about Winston, the owner of this place.'

'That's ridiculous. He's a jerk and the road was never his private property. That's what all this is about.'

Rosemary glanced down at her manicured nails and then up at Claire. 'According to him, Tessa called him a dick. To his face.'

'What does it matter what she did or didn't call him?' Claire asked. 'Of course he hates Tessa. He hates me too, for that matter.'

'Did you call him a dick as well?'

'That's not the point. He hates us because we and the activism we inspired are probably the reasons he is trying to sell the driving range. It was just a matter of time before the state ordered him to stop claiming public property as his own.'

'She was out here.' Rosemary's glossed lips pressed together. 'With Timothy.'

'What are you talking about?' Claire glanced outside just as Eric's car pulled in front of the entrance. 'Timothy works with her. He works with all of us.'

Rosemary shook her head. 'Except Tessa and Timothy weren't working. They were out there on the river bluffs, alone together at night.'

At the entrance, Eric got out of the car, opened the passenger door for Tessa and gave her a quick kiss. Wearing sunglasses and her chili-pepper apron over a black turtleneck and jeans, she walked toward the clubhouse.

'That's absolutely ridiculous. Winston will say anything he thinks will make us look bad.' Claire couldn't continue the argument, not now. She just had to save Tessa from whatever Rosemary was planning.

She rushed to the front door just as Tessa paused and waved to the smattering of cyclists waiting outside the clubhouse.

'Hey,' Tessa said, and gave Claire a quick hug.

'Rosemary's trying to cause trouble,' she whispered. 'I'm going to start the pancakes until the rest of the volunteers arrive.'

'No, you're not.' Tessa took off her sunglasses and met Claire's gaze.

'She's looking for anything to go wrong,' Claire said. 'Let me handle the cooking. You charm the crowd.'

Rosemary got up from her stool and glared at them as if threatening to break up their conversation.

'I can handle it.' Tessa pulled her apron tighter. 'Have I ever told you about my mother's pancakes? She was a really great cook, you know.'

'Tessa,' Claire said, 'Rosemary's raising hell because you left the snakes at that school yesterday. Let me help you, just in case something goes wrong.'

'What could go wrong?' Tessa paused and then glanced over at Rosemary. Then she leaned back out of the door and called to the cyclists. 'Anybody hungry?'

They cheered and Claire started to relax. Maybe cooking was one of those things Tessa didn't have to think about, something she had been doing so long it was second nature.

Another car pulled into the lot.

'Al,' Tessa said. 'Did you know he was coming?'

'No.' Claire pretended to straighten the orange juice glasses.

'Are you OK?' That was pure Tessa, worrying about her when she was the one Claire was trying to help.

As if she knew they had been talking about her, Rosemary crossed the room. 'You'd better hurry,' she told Tessa, as if she were in charge of the event.

Al walked inside in shorts and a plaid shirt Claire hadn't seen before. 'I thought you might need some help,' he said.

She flushed. 'I think we've got it covered.'

'And I thought all volunteers were welcome.'

She wasn't about to ask him why he was really there.

'I guess you can help serve.' Tessa dismissed him with a shrug and walked over to the mixer.

Claire looked at him in the soft morning light – a man with glasses and brown hair, neither tall nor short. And Tessa seemed eager to keep her distance from him.

A group of crows flew overhead. Their cries sent a shiver through Claire.

The rest of the cooking crew arrived. Visitors, most of them on foot, crowded inside around the stove facing the window.

Soon, ten to fifteen people stood admiring the misty view of the river.

'Smells great,' she told Tessa. The bicycle riders sat on benches outside, clutching their cups of coffee.

Claire watched over the batter in the slowly turning bowl of the giant mixer.

'It's better if you blend it by hand,' Tessa said. 'You'll get more air in it that way.'

'It will be fine.' Claire poured the contents of the bowl into the large plastic pitcher and handed it to her.

Tessa only stared. The strips of bacon on the right side of the griddle sizzled and began to shrink.

'Tessa.' Claire nudged her as the smell of burning bacon filled the air.

Oblivious to her confusion, a few volunteers poured orange and cranberry juice while more visitors lined up, waiting.

Finally, Tessa tipped the pitcher and a stream of batter pooled onto the griddle. The mixture sputtered and stuck to the surface. Tessa gazed at it and then at the spatula in her hand.

'What's wrong?' Rosemary asked Claire.

'I think the griddle's too hot,' Tessa said.

The pancakes started to blacken around the edges. Tessa just stared at them.

Claire eased the spatula out of her hand and started turning them. She shoveled two on a plate, added a piece of crisp bacon and handed the plate to Rosemary. 'Next?' she asked, and two more women came forward. Rosemary had no choice but to step back.

Without moving, Al observed it all.

Tessa stared at her hand still in the air. Tears filled her eyes.

'Don't worry,' Claire whispered. 'We'll get through this.'

Just then a stinking hot smell shot through her nostrils. 'Claire?' Tessa looked at her and then down at the pitcher she had placed on the pan of bacon grease. It seemed to collapse into the flames. 'Claire,' Tessa repeated, louder this time.

Claire grabbed the pitcher and ran, carrying it through the back door. The melting plastic smell combined with burning bacon was nauseating. Claire placed it on the ground, grabbed a hose and turned the faucet on full blast. Whatever was wrong with Tessa had just escalated.

The rising sun shone through the windows, blinding her view of the parking lot. She had to clean up this mess before it drove people away and made Tessa look even worse than she already did.

'I'll do that.' Al stepped outside.

'The fire's out.' She let him take the hose and the pan of grease. 'But the smell.'

'I turned on the fans. Nothing else we can do about that.' He glanced at the door. 'Tessa's pretty upset.'

'I've got to get back to her.'

She ran inside, where Tessa stood before a group of expectant volunteers. Rosemary was not among them. Everyone else had moved outside, mumbling and speaking among themselves in front of the building.

'I can finish cooking,' Claire told her. 'You help the others serve orange juice.'

Tessa stared straight ahead, the way she had when she had forgotten what to do with the spatula. 'Orange juice.'

'That's right.'

Tessa nodded. She took off the apron and placed it on the counter. 'How?' she asked.

'The glasses are stacked on the table there. You will fill them from one of those.' Claire pointed at the pitchers beside the glasses. 'Then the people will pick them up.'

'I can do that.'

As Claire cooked, Tessa moved through the crowd, pouring juice, smiling. Al opened the front door and the horrible smell gradually dissipated. It did not disappear entirely, though. As Claire went through the motions of cooking, he stood beside her, helping serve, handing her ingredients.

As the crowd began to disperse, Tessa stood outside with the cyclists, carrying on a lively conversation.

From the window, Claire saw Rosemary watching from the porch.

'She won't leave Tessa alone,' she told Al under her breath.

'What was wrong with Tessa?' he asked.

'I don't know. Please don't say anything to anyone.' Claire handed him the empty pitcher and he filled it.

Rosemary entered the clubhouse and started toward them. 'Oh, great,' he said.

'Hello, Al.' Rosemary approached the griddle. 'Helping out?'

'Trying to.'

'I'm surprised,' she said in a pleasant tone. 'Considering they found your gun out here and all.'

'I don't know if it was my gun, and since I don't have anything to do with what happened to it, there's no reason I shouldn't be out here.' He slammed the pitcher on the counter. 'You know, I'm willing to handle your graphics because I care about the river and the conservancy. That can change at any time.'

Rosemary's cheeks flushed, but she just shrugged without responding to him.

'This can't go on,' she said to Claire. 'Someone could have gotten hurt here today.'

'But no one did.' People began lining up and Claire lowered her voice. 'Besides, this is something that should be discussed at another time.'

'Oh, it will be,' Rosemary said.

ELEVEN

Tessa

Although Tessa has tried to avoid looking at herself all morning, wherever she glances – the mirrored cabinet in her bedroom, the forgotten compact on the bureau, even the shower door – she sees her face everywhere. Her eyes are as deceiving and unreliable as glass. She made a fool of herself out there – a public fool, as her mother would say.

She avoids Eric all day, which isn't that difficult considering that he is spending every possible moment on the Gloria Sudbury case. Avoiding Claire is more difficult, but Tessa pulls that off too by not answering her phone or looking at her text messages. Still, as busy as Eric is, he is always the first to hear anything going on, and he probably already knows what happened at the pancake breakfast.

She's taken time with her makeup and hair just in case. She has sneaked out behind drawn drapes into the kitchen and recreated the scampi recipe Eric swears made him fall in love with her. Frozen shrimp from Trader Joe's, but he won't know the difference. He never has. Hers is better than what they had with Claire in that restaurant at Christmas. What was the name of that place?

The house smells of garlic and her cedar wood candle, and when Eric walks in the side door from the garage, he stops and, just like that, the tension in his face begins to ease.

'Tess,' he says. 'You've done it again.'

He removes his suit jacket and throws his tie over the back of his chair, a gesture she loves. They have an early, easy dinner, with one glass each of a good cabernet, and as she clears the table Eric starts upstairs to take care of 'loose ends,' as he calls them.

'Don't forget dessert.' Her laughter isn't a giggle – something lower than that and rich with promise.

'Maybe just coffee.' He returns to the counter, pats her behind, smiles and gives her a kiss on the cheek. 'I'll collect on the dessert tomorrow morning.'

Tessa smiles back at him. She knows how he likes mornings.

His phone dings. 'More on Gloria Sudbury,' he says. 'Sorry, Tess. Love you.' He kisses her cheek again and walks outside, closing the patio door behind him.

Tessa cleans up the last of the dishes. She should make the scampi more often. She should remind Eric of herself more often, too.

The outdoor light to the left of the kitchen is turned on and it looks like yellow fog highlighting the side yard. Tessa walks over and looks out. Finally, they are getting some rain. Should she pull out the sweet potatoes she put in last spring? She studies the chives and mint leaves mingled in one of her rain-soaked earth boxes. Then she sees the image of her bare feet through the windows, her toenails superimposed on the gray pebbles outside. She feels the round shapes of the small rocks under her feet, and it's as if she is standing on those rocks and not here on the tile floor of her own kitchen.

Tessa steps back from the image. There's the proof in front of her. You can appear to be one place, on round, hard pebbles, for instance, when you are really somewhere else. Could that poor woman on the river be the same way?

As she stands there, the sound of Eric's muffled voice comes through the glass.

'I don't care what she did. I'm not going to subject her to a bunch of humiliating tests . . . I said I don't care. I'll pay for the repairs. It's not as if she burned something down.'

So Eric does know what happened at the pancake breakfast. Of course he knows.

'Try to keep your eye on her for now. If anything, spend more time with her, get her to open up to you.'

A pause and then, 'I understand that, but sometimes we have to put differences aside.'

Tessa wants to cover her ears but she can't. Eric is speaking to someone he trusts, someone who knows about her.

'Would you really want her to go through those tests? What do you mean? I don't care if there's damage, or how much damage for that matter. I'll make sure she has all the care she needs right here. Thanks for understanding. Maybe we could meet. The usual time?'

Tessa cannot move. He's talking to someone about her in that soft voice he uses when he's addressing women on a jury. The scrape of the door to her right sends a chill through her and she refuses to look around. Eric closes the door and, still holding his phone, comes over to her.

'Whatcha doing?' he asks.

'Just looking out there at the pebbles.' She turns and forces herself to smile up into his eyes. 'What were *you* doing?'

'Talking to a friend.'

'About me?'

'Of course not.' His courtroom voice takes over the conversation. 'Why would you say that?'

'Because I did something awful yesterday,' she tells him. 'I was making pancakes at the fundraiser and I guess I forgot where I put the batter.'

'That's no big deal.' He drapes an arm over her shoulder. 'You don't need that job anyway. Why don't you quit?'

Looking into his eyes the way she studied her reflection on the pebbles, she realizes she has never considered that option. 'But what would I do, Eric?'

'Gloria Sudbury has taken up sketching. She's doing some nice work, actually.'

'Gloria Sudbury is in a jail cell.'

'That's not what I meant,' Eric says.

She stares out at the pebbles again. 'I'm not going to take up sketching.'

'All right, then. It was just a suggestion.' He heads toward the stairs and looks back at her. 'I need to go back to the office for an hour or so. You get some rest.'

'I will,' she says. Once the garage door lifts and his car pulls out, Tessa knows where she will go.

Claire

Tessa had suffered some kind of breakdown when she'd attempted to cook the pancakes. Rosemary had witnessed it, and she would use what she had seen to try to get rid of Tessa. But not if Claire could help it. Something about this mission of Rosemary's didn't compute. Even though Tessa was dealing with problems that needed to be addressed, Rosemary had been uncharacteristically judgmental about her from the start. Natalia, too. When she had attended some of Bobby Glover's charity fundraising events with them when she was married to Al, Claire had found her aloof but not mean. Natalia probably believed whatever lies Rosemary told her about Tessa.

After everyone left the pancake breakfast, Al had helped Claire and the volunteers clean up. He didn't explain what he was doing there, and he didn't say or do anything that could be even remotely perceived as personal.

When he got ready to leave, they walked outside, picking up paper cups and plates, and Claire finally had an opportunity to speak to him.

'I need to ask you this,' she said.

He nodded. 'About what happened in there?'

'Can we keep it quiet? Tessa doesn't need anymore stress right now.'

'I have no reason to say anything,' Al said. 'Rosemary will, though.' He finished filling a large trash bag and looked over at Claire as if deciding whether or not to speak.

They used to say they could read each other's minds, and that's how Claire felt just then.

'Tell me,' she said.

He put down the bag and sat at a picnic table. 'You aren't going to believe this, but the Rosemary I used to know was a good person.'

'You're right. I don't believe it.' Claire sat across from him. 'The Rosemary we saw this morning is the one I've been dealing with and she is anything but good. What happened?'

'My divorce,' he said. 'When Natalia left, Rosemary stopped being my friend. Now, ever since the Luger turned up in that car, she's been in attack mode.'

'Just because you divorced her best friend?'

He shook his head and rose from the table. 'Just because her best friend divorced me. I still don't get it.'

Neither did Claire. At least he had agreed not to talk about what happened at the pancake breakfast. Most of those attending had no idea exactly what went wrong. Almost all of them had been outside, and the few who had to deal with the smoke didn't seem to connect it to Tessa's burning plastic.

Early in the morning, before the others arrived, they moved the rest of their office to the university. Tessa seemed subdued, and Claire could tell she was too humiliated to discuss what had happened. They had to discuss it, though. Tessa needed to get help, to find out what was causing her memory loss.

The weather report predicted midday showers and they had both dressed for it, Tessa in a cropped hoodie Claire couldn't remember seeing before. Dark clouds bunched together overhead and they hurried inside. The sting of smoke still drifted over from the clubhouse and hung in the air. Partitions had been moved, yet the shell of the office remained. A few boxes were stacked on what used to be Tessa's desk, which now faced the front window overlooking the parking lot and the bluffs where Timothy had dragged the mangled car out of the water more than a month ago now. The same water where she and Tessa had discovered the body of a dead woman.

Some other nonprofit would move in here – maybe not right away but as soon as whatever was or wasn't discovered here had been resolved. Again, Claire thought of Al, as she did every time she looked at the river now. He had been her friend before, during and after his marriage, and he had momentarily been her lover. If he had been holding back anything about the gun, surely she would sense it. But she still couldn't figure out why he had shown up at the breakfast. Why had he come? Claire wanted to think it was to see her, but if that had been the case, he wouldn't have left after helping her clean up.

'What are you thinking?' Tessa joined her at the window and they stared at the landscape blurred by river fog.

'About how vivid it is out there in spite of the cloud cover.'

'Not about how I made an ass out of myself on Saturday?' Tessa picked up her hat from the desk and pulled it over her head. Her playful smile reminded Claire of how she had looked the day they reconnected, but behind that smile and those blue eyes she didn't seem like the same woman.

'No, and you didn't,' Claire said. 'To tell you the truth, I was thinking about what Danny said when we had that little exchange in his office. He accused me of being a poor judge of people and, even though he meant Al, it wasn't the first time he'd accused me of that.'

'I think you're a great judge.' Tessa picked up a box from the desk. 'You're just a poor judge of husbands.'

'Maybe.' She grabbed the handle of the cart stacked with the three remaining cartons. 'Aren't you glad we're getting out of here?'

Tessa didn't move. 'He called me, by the way,' she said.

'Danny?'

She nodded. 'He wanted to go to lunch and I hung up on him.' She broke into a grin.

'You didn't,' Claire said. 'He called you because I asked him to.'

'Why would you do that?' Still holding the box, Tessa leaned against the desk. 'He left a message saying he was just checking up on me. Why would you need him to do that when you see me almost every day?'

'That's not how it happened,' Claire said. 'It was that time I told you about, when Amanda, his assistant, was there.'

'What does that have to do with him pretending to reach out to me?'

'I was worried about you,' Claire said. 'Come on. Let's get out of here, OK?'

Tessa crossed her arms. 'Not until you tell me the truth about why you talked to Danny about me.'

'All right.' Claire didn't have a choice. 'I told you I was worried after we went to San Francisco that day.'

'So you told Danny that I had forgotten for one second that Wally was dead?'

'I was also worried once they pulled the car out and you told me you saw someone on the river,' Claire said. 'I thought you and Danny were in touch because of the flying lessons he was giving Jake.'

'That was between Jake and him.' She sighed and headed for the door. 'Don't talk to Danny about me anymore, all right?'

'We haven't spoken since then and we probably won't again.'
Claire dragged the cart outside. 'I'm sorry.' She stopped and
looked back at the structure that had once seemed like the
ideal place in the ideal setting for her job. 'Maybe you ought
to see a doctor,' she said. 'Just get checked out.'

'Because?' Tessa laughed but her fists were clenched.
'Because I forgot where I placed some pancake batter?'

'Because sometimes you forget things. I care about you,
Tessa. Whatever it is, we'll figure it out.'

'Figure what out?' Her voice dropped to a whisper.

'Hey,' Claire said. 'Everyone needs a medical opinion now
and then. It was just a suggestion.'

'One I'm not taking.'

'At least think about it,' she said. 'Please.'

Tessa leaned against the doorframe. 'Maybe you ought to
think about a few things yourself.'

'Come on,' Claire said. 'This isn't helping anything.'

'Of course it's not.' Tessa looked up at her. 'I burned some
pancakes, Claire. It's been too long since I tried to cook them.
Is that any worse than what you've done?'

But Claire didn't forget things. She would not have put
down a plastic pitcher on a hot grill. She glanced back at
Tessa and said, 'I'm not telling you what to do. I'm just
saying . . .'

'That I need to get a checkup to be sure my mind's OK?'
Tessa stood in the doorway, unsmiling. 'And you're sure that's
your idea? That you came up with it all by yourself?'

'Of course it's my idea, and it's not a bad one. Ever since
they found that car, the situation out here has been stressful.'

Tessa crossed the room, and when they were close enough
to touch, said, 'Just tell me one thing.'

'What?' Claire asked.

'Have you been talking to Eric?'

'No, of course not.' She felt herself flush. How could Tessa
think that? 'I told you that I haven't shared anything with
him.'

For a couple of seconds, neither of them spoke and Claire
fought the impulse to look away. Finally, she said, 'You know
I'm telling you the truth. Please think about it.'

'I will.' Tessa shrugged and headed toward the car. 'Let's just get the rest of this office moved.'

Claire knew she wouldn't be able to get through to her just now. Tessa didn't believe she had a problem, and if Claire pushed she would only create more tension between them. Better to just get moved in and hope they could finish the job together without interruption. She and Tessa often communicated best when they were doing simple tasks. Maybe the act of moving would bring them close enough that Claire could help Tessa realize she needed to get checked out.

When they pulled into the parking place closest to their new office at the university, Claire saw Rosemary standing outside, leaning against her car, and they sighed in unison.

'The last thing we need,' Tessa said.

Claire nodded and tried to sound positive. 'Let's deal with her before we take this stuff inside. We're going to have to, sooner or later.'

'I am so not in the mood.' Tessa didn't bother to lower her voice. 'What do you think she's doing here so early?'

Claire knew why she was there, and she could tell from her folded arms pressed against her black raincoat that Rosemary was out for blood.

'The Devil never sleeps,' she said.

Tessa giggled the way she used to, as if nothing could stifle her exuberance. 'Then let's go butt heads,' she said.

'Hey, Rosemary,' Claire said as she joined them at the car. 'You're up early.'

Rosemary was bareheaded for once, her hair slicked back like a glistening black cap against her head. 'I had a feeling I'd find both of you here,' she said.

'We're moving in the last of the stuff,' Tessa shot back. 'Want to help us unpack?'

In that instant, Tessa's voice sounded like Eric's – not the tone, but the certainty and the challenge in it.

Rosemary stopped where she stood, and Claire paused as well.

'That's not why I'm here.' Rosemary cleared her throat. 'I came because we need to discuss what went wrong at the pancake breakfast.'

'Nothing went wrong. We made a profit.' Claire turned to Tessa. 'Didn't we?'

'You better believe we did.'

'And you could have burned down the whole place.'

'With bacon grease? Actually, you're lucky I didn't, Rosemary, considering the way you were breathing down my neck.' Tessa marched ahead of them toward the greenhouses.

Claire hurried next to her, wondering how to stop the barrage of words if Tessa got really angry. Her strident tone was the same as the day she'd informed Winston that he and his golf-club members were 'dicks with sticks.'

'I *had* to breathe down your neck, as you put it.' Rosemary kept up with them, her voice tight and tense. 'You left snakes at an elementary school.'

'Harmless snakes,' Claire put in.

Rosemary waved her away and continued to glare at Tessa. 'Not only that, but you're acting unprofessionally, meeting Timothy after hours.'

Claire expected Tessa to deny it. Instead, she laughed. 'So, what are you?' She leaned against the greenhouse door and looked Rosemary's thin body up and down. 'The chastity patrol?'

Claire bit back a gasp. Rosemary swallowed so hard that the veins in her throat bulged.

'Don't think . . .' She spoke slowly, enunciating each word carefully. 'Don't think I'm going to stay silent about this.'

A raindrop hit Claire's face and a few more drops followed. She wiped her eyes.

'So we had a little problem with the griddle on Saturday,' Claire said. 'Tell anyone anything you like. But while you're doing that, check out how many new members we signed up at the pancake breakfast.'

'You're as guilty as she is,' Rosemary said.

Tessa hurried inside to get out of the rain and closed the door behind her.

Now it was just Claire, Rosemary and the rain. Claire breathed in the misty air. 'Guilty how?' she asked.

'Because you know the truth and you're trying to hide it.' Rosemary wiped off raindrops from her forehead. 'There's something wrong with Tessa.'

'That's ridiculous.' Claire reached for the door to her office. 'If you'd like to call a board meeting, I'd be happy to discuss it.'

'Maybe that's a good idea,' Rosemary said, but her lips were tight and Claire could tell that she had managed to distract her.

'Do whatever you like,' Claire said. 'In the meantime, I need to get back to work.'

She closed the door behind her before this got worse, and wondered how much of it she should share with Tessa.

TWELVE

Tessa

So she left a snake cage in a classroom, Tessa thinks. The world hasn't stopped. No one has been harmed. Although Rosemary might try to make a big deal out of it, no one else will care. The snakes are probably less harmful than Rosemary is.

As she pictures their overly made-up manager with the features of a snake, Tessa stifles a giggle. She's glad they finally got moved into the greenhouse complex at the university. She's glad Claire practically slammed the door in Rosemary's face. Most of all, though, she's glad that Claire defended her, especially after what she said earlier about doctors and checkups.

A snake cage. A few burned pancakes. It isn't the end of the world. Yet, as Tessa turns on the TV and stands in her living room, something makes her feel jumpy, as if she's had too much coffee, too much something. She thinks about the figure in the ice-blue dress on the river again and wonders how you can save someone you're not sure is real.

Eric's face covers every local channel on the television. To Tessa, he looks like a handsome stranger. His image seems to shimmer. Depending on how the light hits him, his expression is brilliant, compassionate, outraged. At one point, when he turns to face the camera, she can see the glint of tears, or maybe it's a trick of the light.

Gloria Sudbury, on the other hand, wearing a coat so long and drab it could be from a silent movie, clutches her hands and stares down at them. Her dark hair is twisted into a tight knot at the back of her neck. Most of the shots of her are exactly the same, as if she has only one position – hands in lap, and then that slow, upward, ultimately defiant glance into the camera. Finally, she lifts her large, dark eyes and dares the viewers to witness her misery. Some of this is what Eric calls his choreography, of course. But most of what Tessa sees in Gloria Sudbury's face here, in her own house, on her own television, is pain no one could fake.

'The poor woman.' She realizes she has said it aloud and places her fingers over her lips.

This is what Eric wants people to feel. He knows how to create an image of this once-lovely woman's life. He has painted her in fragile black and white, with just that lifted gaze and final eye contact, that quick glimpse of what anyone might look like after she has been pushed, tormented and tortured to the point of murder. Forget the fact that Gloria's husband was asleep at the time. That is not the issue. The only issue that matters is the sorrowful light in this woman's eyes.

Considering his late meeting with Bobby Glover at the TV station, Eric probably won't be home until after eleven. Maybe later. Tessa should probably make a toddy and go to bed. Where did that come from? Her mother? She wouldn't know how to make a toddy if she had to. She doesn't even like to drink other than a glass of wine now and then, and she has no tolerance for the out-of-control partying she has watched her friends, even Claire that one time, succumb to. That night and those drinks had changed Claire in a way. They have made her more secretive.

Tessa picks up the remote from the back of the sofa where Eric must have left it and switches off the television. Her body moves, as if by its own volition, toward the double doors of her patio. She feels as if she is gliding across the room without any way to stop, but she doesn't need to stop. She has time.

She steps out onto the path to her right, away from the railroad tracks, back toward the darkness. Across the river, another town is painted in ghostlike images with ground fog like the low-traveling tangle of mist she got lost in that night she left Claire and Eric alone in the car when she ran back to the office to retrieve her purse.

If she takes this long, loop-shaped path all the way around, toward and then away from the railroad tracks, she will end up here thirty or forty minutes later in the same spot. She could also get in trouble this time of night. The Whole Foods shopping cart against the fence to her left hasn't moved since the last time she was out here late, but that doesn't mean she is alone.

Tessa pretends she is exercising – yoga, maybe. Pilates, childbirth. Breathe in. Breathe out. And with that exhale, make your move.

In.

Out.

'Timothy?' The breathing exercise has left her dizzy. 'Are you here?'

Leaves squish. 'I'm here.' Timothy trudges down the uphill path to her left, closer to the train tracks. His boots make a sucking sound in the mud as he tries to keep his balance. In moments, he is beside her, and Tessa is so relieved that she almost hugs him.

'Are you out here every night?' she asks and starts walking toward the street.

'Just when I need to be.' His voice is more guarded than usual, as if he has secrets of his own. An image flashes into her mind, and Tessa wonders if he too watched Eric on television tonight. 'Are you all right?' Timothy asks.

'I'm fine.' She steps under the streetlight and gives him a smile to prove it.

'Why'd you come then?'

'I don't know.' She glances down at her hands and hates the way they look, especially compared to the way Gloria Sudbury's looked on television. 'Maybe I was lonely.'

'I'll drive you home,' he says. 'My truck's not far from here.' He can't seem to meet her eyes.

She moves closer to him, the way she would to a child. 'What's wrong?' she asks.

He shakes his head and turns away from her.

'What's wrong, Timothy?'

'I'll drive you home,' he says. 'That's all I can do right now, OK?'

She nods because she knows that once she is in the truck with him she can ask more questions. Timothy can't resist her questions for long. It's as if he's drawn to them, to her.

The road from the river to her home seems longer than usual. Tessa reaches out and touches his sleeve.

'I'm scared,' she says. Then she shrinks back against the seat in his pickup and wishes she could take it back. 'Probably just a long day. It's been a long day, all right.'

Timothy nods and drives straight ahead. Soon she recognizes her street.

Just before her house, he pulls the truck to the curb. They sit there for a moment, and finally he turns to her as if ready to get out and open the passenger door the way he likes to do with her when she gets out a few houses down. Instead, he says, 'Me too.'

Tessa's back flattens against the seat. 'Why?'

'I can't tell you. It might scare you even more.'

'And you think what you just said didn't do that? Tell me, Timothy.'

Finally, Timothy looks over at her. 'I found something,' he says. 'Out there by the river.'

'What?'

'Something that would get me in trouble.' He digs his hands into the pocket of his thick jacket. 'If I give it to you, do you promise me that you'll see that it gets to the right people?'

'What is it? What'd you find?'

'Two things.'

'And what right people do you mean? Eric?'

'I asked you to promise,' he says.

'Of course. I promise, but I need to know what you want me to do.'

His hands in his pocket have turned into fists.

'I can't risk anymore trouble, not right now,' he says. She thinks about Rosemary and her ugly words. 'I just hope I don't cause more trouble for you.'

'Why do you say that?'

'Everything I do at the moment is wrong.'

He turns the key and lowers his window. The cool air blowing into the car makes her realize how flushed her face must be.

'You couldn't have helped that fire,' Timothy says.

'You don't think so?' Other than the smell, it's a blur in

her memory. 'One minute, everything was all right, and the next, it was out of control.'

'It could have happened to anyone.'

'Rosemary said . . .' Her throat tightens and she fights to gets the words out. 'She told Claire there's something wrong with me.'

'That's crazy,' he says. 'What'd Claire say?'

'I don't know.' She stares out of the window at the broken moonlight through the clouds. 'Maybe you should show Claire what you found. She'll know what to do.'

'No.' He says it so sharply that she jumps. 'Sorry,' he says. 'She can't know these came from me. No one can.'

She can't turn him down, not after all the times he's tried to help her when she forgot something she shouldn't have, even when Wally was still alive.

'Then show me,' she says.

Timothy reaches into his jacket and pulls out something pointed that gleams in the light.

She gasps, and then realizes that it's not a knife. 'Just a nail file?' she asks, and takes it from him.

'Yeah, but this is what I found with it.'

He takes out something else and gives it to her. Damp cardboard. Bullets. Tessa doesn't like the metallic smell or the soggy feeling of the package in her hand.

'Where did you get this?' she whispers.

'I told you. The river.'

'But where on the river? The same place you found the car?'

'Close enough.' He seems to study the expression on her face. 'Before I found the car,' he says. 'You see what I mean?'

And Tessa says, 'Yes.'

She takes the soggy box of bullets from Timothy because she can't bear to turn him down. His eyes are too wide with fear, his voice too bumbling and awkward, the way it was when he first started working with Wally. She knows how it feels to question yourself, to assume the problem is you and not them. So, even though she doesn't know what she is going to do, Tessa takes the box and the nail file he found with it and tells him she will make sure it gets to the authorities. One thing is for sure. She can't share it with Claire, not with Claire so worried about Al's involvement.

At work the next day, they continue to finish the move into their offices, so she doesn't have to talk much to Claire except about business. She wants to ask what Claire said to Rosemary but doesn't know how to start the conversation. Claire has a meeting early that afternoon, and she tells Tessa she can leave too. 'We both worked a lot of extra hours over Christmas,' she said, but Tessa can't remember working over Christmas.

Still, she nods and says, 'OK. See you tomorrow.'

As she watches Claire leave, her loose braid resting over the back of her jacket, Tessa realizes that she doesn't have a car. Claire probably thinks that Eric will pick her up, but Tessa can't bother him right now. She could call Timothy, but something makes her want to find her own way for once.

She walks past the greenhouses along the narrow road that borders the agriculture department and the black, rain-soaked furrows that will become corn and grapes later in the year. A little farther down the road, she passes the fake city the college created for recruits – a sprawling but centralized area of restaurants on either side of a city square. When prospective instructors or athletics team members visit to decide if they would like living in Central California, they are taken there for sushi, burgers and steak. They eat ice cream processed at the university and drink local handcrafted beer beside wide windows overlooking elegant student condominium rentals with the foothills to the east and the stadium to the west.

Tessa realizes that she is getting tired and her mind is wandering. But she knows how to get home.

Bus stop, the blue sign on campus says.

She sits down on the bench next to two students, one reading, one texting. Others approach, some sitting beside the bench and some leaning against the structure, bracing it on either side. When the bus pulls up, they will all board.

She knows how to get home. One transfer and then another. She remembers how people on a bus pretend others are invisible. Or they pretend to be asleep. Or they act as if a heavy suitcase or shoulder bag in the seat beside them is another person, so that a real person won't sit down.

Tessa doesn't care about that, but she's happy when she finds an empty seat next to a window. She overhears snatches of conversations and isn't sure if they're real. A man and a woman who just met talk about the friends they have in common, only they don't have any.

Tessa is relieved and eager to be on the road, away from Fresno, which is really at least five towns. There is Ignored Downtown Fresno, once a shopping mall, now a sprawl of torn-up streets frequented by homeless people, many of whom have been driven from homeless camps. There is Invisible Westside Fresno, where the blacks were shoved years before and left to survive or not. Farther north, there is Fig Garden Fresno, which had once been real fig trees and is now a cluster of mid-century modern homes and people to match gathered around a Whole Foods market. Farther northeast, there is Gated Community Fresno, where most non-natives with money live overlooking Clorox lakes, and where Eric had once considered moving them. And then, both east and west, there is River Bluffs Fresno, the homes close enough to the San Joaquin River so that those who live there can breathe that cool morning air, even before the temperatures climb in summer. Tessa is glad she lives there. Still, she needs to get somewhere else right now, some kind of other home, her home.

The bus driver, a short woman with a powerful voice and windshields so enormous they look safe, guides them down Highway 99, past Kingsburg and the RV Park along the Kings River, past the off-ramps. She knows the names of these towns, knows them like a poem.

Delano.

McFarland.

Wasco.

Shafter.

Bakersfield.

She knows to get off before Shafter, just like always. The line is short, only two people in front of her. Once off the bus, she stands under the cloudy sky and tries to find her sense of direction.

'Hey.' A girl about the same age as those kids at the bus stop says, 'You need some help?'

'Just going home,' Tessa tells her. 'I'm fine.'

'You better hurry. It's about to rain.'

'I need to rent a car.'

The girl points, and Tessa hurries in that direction. Once she's inside, she grins at the clerk in front of her, who seems happy in his small quarters with the tinkle of raindrops against the glass. All he wants is ID, a license, a credit card. Easy enough.

Finally, Tessa drives. It's not that late, just overcast because of the spreading clouds. She doesn't have to think. The streets lead her. Now, here she is. Better to park in front. Someone might need the driveway.

She gets out and smooths the front of her shirt, more wrinkled from travel than she realized. For a moment, she wonders if she slept on the last bus. Tessa walks up to the front door and into her house. Only the door is locked. She looks at the brick pillars on each side and runs her fingers between the bricks to find her key, only it isn't there. She panics. She needs to find it.

Before she can, the front door opens.

Tessa squints through the screen. Gardenia perfume and cigarette smoke drift out. She can see the outline of her mother behind the screen.

'What are you doing here?'

'Hi, Mom. What happened to my key?'

'Give me a minute.'

Tessa hears rustling and wonders why it should be so difficult to enter her own home. 'Mom,' she calls out.

'I said give me a minute. Please.'

Tessa stands outside, trying to see her mother, their home. Finally, the door opens and her mother stands there in black tights and a kind of green tunic.

'About time,' Tessa says. 'Are you all right?'

'Oh, I'm fine.' Her mother walks past her to the step-down kitchen with its black-and-white tile, and Tessa follows. 'You hungry?'

Tessa thinks about pancakes and shakes her head. 'I just got a little overwhelmed.'

'Like you forgot you told all your friends your mother was dead?'

As Tessa looks at her mother's dark hair, so thick that it falls over one eyebrow, she remembers, and she is ashamed.

'It was easier that way.'

'To say your mother's dead is easier? She puts her hands on her hips and Tessa remembers how she used to stand like that. 'You're getting more like your father every day.'

Tessa feels herself flush. 'What do you mean by that?'

'You know what I mean.' She taps a fingernail against her head.

'I'm not.' Tessa's breathing quickens. 'And I didn't mean to bother you. I was thinking about your pancakes, and I might have gotten mixed up.'

'Are you going to punish me for those pancakes for the rest of my life?'

'That's not what I mean.'

'Of course it's what you mean.' Her mother picks up one of two coffee mugs off the counter, and Tessa wonders who the other one is for. 'You tell people I'm dead. You blame me for having no money when your crazy deadbeat father had custody of you. Yes, I made you pay for breakfast, but it was his money and he owed it to me.'

You charged me for breakfast. At home. Ten dollars. Tessa remembers now. That's what she's come here for. To remember.

'Thanks, Mom,' she says. 'I need to get back.'

'Not so fast.' She picks up a phone off the counter. Then she moves past Tessa and stands between her and the door. Glaring at her, she speaks into her phone. 'Come get your wife.'

Eric. Her mother has actually called Eric. Tessa pushes her aside and runs through the door.

THIRTEEN

Claire

Claire tried to call Tessa later that day but she didn't pick up. Claire shouldn't have brushed off Rosemary's attack, most of which Tessa had to have heard. Maybe she should call Eric, but she had promised Tessa she wouldn't share anything with him. Regardless, she needed to find out where Tessa was.

As Claire drove along the bluffs, she realized that Tessa probably wasn't home. She turned off onto Tessa's street anyway and sat there for a few minutes, trying to put off the moment and yet knowing she couldn't. As always, the striking silhouettes of the trees enhanced the lush landscaping and pillars of irregular river rock. Yet the setting, a blend of peach, pink and gray, failed to calm her.

Eric's car sat in the drive, a good sign. He came out of the side door just as she approached.

'Claire. Hey. Where's Tess?'

Claire stopped as he approached her. 'I was hoping I'd find her here.'

'I tried to call her but she didn't pick up.' He pulled his phone out of his pocket and looked down at the screen. 'Oh, crap. A message from Eleanor.'

The voicemail clicked on. 'Come get your wife.' A low-pitched, unemotional woman's voice.

Eric played it again. 'Come get your wife.'

Clutching the phone, he looked at Claire.

'Who is that?' she asked.

'Eleanor.' He bit his lip. 'Tessa's mother.'

'I thought her mother was dead.'

'Only to Tess.' He lifted the phone as if it were a heavy weight in his hand. 'I'd better call her back.'

Claire watched him place the call, trying to make sense out of the stories Tessa had told her about her dead mother.

'Hey, Eleanor. Eric, here. I got your message and I'm on my way. Don't let her leave. I'll be there as soon as I can, probably around five or five-thirty. Again, do not let her leave. Please call back if that's possible.'

'Where is she?' Claire asked.

'South of here, near Wasco, between there and Bakersfield.'

'I'm going with you.'

'She won't want you to see her mother or the way she lives.'

He started toward the car and Claire followed him. 'We're way past that, Eric.'

That got a short laugh out of him. 'All right,' he said. 'Let's go.'

The car smelled clean with a hint of citrus, like him. Eric drove to the end of the street and then turned left, parallel with the train tracks, heading toward the highway.

'When was the last time you saw her, Claire?'

With that voice, that gaze, he could get Gloria Sudbury or anyone else off on a murder charge. His question was that perfectly phrased.

'Today. She left early.' The simple statement felt like a betrayal.

'What time?'

'Around eleven-thirty, I'd say.'

'Any mention of where she was going?'

'None. I thought you were picking her up,' Claire said. 'I shouldn't have left her there.'

'It wasn't your fault. Have you checked your phone?'

She nodded. 'I'll look again.'

'Send her a text, will you?'

Her head still spinning with questions about where Tessa was and why she had done this, Claire did as Eric asked.

Tessa, please let me know you're OK. I'll find you wherever you are.

She would, too.

Eric drove fast, shooting past the small towns on Highway 99. As he gained on a long, swerving truck, it started to move into their lane and Claire gripped the sides of her seat.

Eric honked his horn and the truck drifted back to the right.

'Don't worry,' he told her. 'I'm a good driver. Besides, I'll slow down once we're out of this traffic. In the meantime, what can you tell me about what's happened to upset my wife like this?'

'I don't know,' she said, still holding onto her seat.

'You need to level with me.' Although he glanced at her only briefly, Claire felt as if she were in a courtroom.

'It's Rosemary,' she said.

'That bitch.' He passed another truck and stayed in the fast lane this time.

Claire turned in the seat and studied his profile. 'Do you know about the accident at the pancake breakfast?'

'Of course I know,' he said. 'Rosemary couldn't wait to call me. I offered to pay for any damage and tried to talk Tessa into quitting the job.'

'That's not a good idea,' Claire said. 'She needs it.'

'Well, she doesn't need this.' He waved at the expanse of highway as if the traffic and the weather were the cause of Tessa's problems.

'Except for the pressure from Rosemary, the job is good for her,' she said.

He sighed and kept his eyes on the road. 'I also know she left the snakes in a school classroom, too.'

Claire felt as if she'd been caught in a lie. 'Timothy picked them up that same afternoon,' she said. 'No harm done.'

'Maybe not then, but what about the next time? Rosemary was right to be alarmed.'

'She wasn't alarmed,' Claire said. 'She was picking on Tessa, putting her under even more stress.'

They were now passing every vehicle on their right, and Eric moved closer behind an SUV in their lane. 'Maybe all she needs is a leave of absence.'

'What would she do all day?' Claire said.

'Rest for a change. Catch up on her sleep. Maybe take up a hobby.' He focused on the car ahead of them as if willing it into the next lane. 'This morning she woke up talking to that imaginary woman again. When I tried to get her attention, she didn't even recognize me at first.'

'Sometimes . . .' Claire couldn't finish the sentence.

Eric honked his horn and the SUV moved into the right-hand lane.

'Sometimes what?'

'Sometimes she's forgetful, I agree. But I don't think quitting her job or even taking a leave of absence is going to make her better. She probably needs to see a doctor.'

'I'm not putting her through that humiliation,' he said. 'She's terrified of being like her father.'

'Being like him how?'

'Early-onset dementia.'

'Tessa never mentioned that,' Claire told him. 'All she shared with me was that he raised her.'

'Until he couldn't anymore, and she had to take care of him. Watching him decline was really hard on her. I'm not going to force her to take a slew of tests.'

'Everyone gets checkups, and a lot of treatable health issues can cause memory problems.' Eric didn't respond, and Claire knew he was considering it. 'Maybe just start with a physical exam,' she said.

'That might be a possibility. But I still think she's under too much pressure on the job.'

'Only because of Rosemary,' Claire agreed. 'She hates Tessa.'

'Why?'

'I have no idea, but she has hated her from the beginning. Natalia hates her too.'

'I've never seen any evidence of that, and I've known Rosemary since back when she was working in law herself.' His laugh was short. 'She's nasty to everyone.'

'But she's worse to Tessa, especially now.'

'Another reason she needs to get away from there.' She started to object and he added, 'At least for a while. Isn't Rosemary supposed to be starting an environmental consulting firm?'

'Supposedly, she's talked to Natalia about going in together once Natalia's back in the country.'

'And that's not so far away, is it?' he asked. 'Tessa could certainly take a month or two off and wait for Rosemary to move on.'

'I think it might be a setback for her,' she said. 'I really do.'

'You're a tough one.' He signaled, moved into the right lane and then took the turnoff. At the stoplight, he shook his head and smiled at her. 'I hope I never get you on a jury.'

'I care about Tessa,' she said.

'I know that.' He squeezed her arm. 'She's had a lot of admirers as long as I've known her, but you might be her first friend.'

'I doubt that, Eric.'

'Oh, really?' he said. 'Tell me, how many of those women are coming around now?'

She thought back to Tessa's onetime friends in their gray, pink and blue. The cashmere women. 'She has the volunteers, the schools, the daycare center and the Green Thumbs.'

'Those are the people she gives to.'

'They make her feel worthwhile.'

'And so do you,' he told her. 'Maybe you're right about the job.'

'I am, Eric,' she said.

'I don't know. I'm just desperate. About ready to win the biggest case of my career, and I don't even know where my wife is.'

'We will find her,' she said.

Tessa would contact her soon. Whatever had happened wasn't so bad that it couldn't be fixed.

'Thank you.' The light changed and he made a left-hand turn. 'Thank you for being in her life,' he said, and his voice broke. 'And thank you for being in mine.'

Tessa

The lights on the highway come in flashes. She will be all right. She just needs to get back.

Where is back? It is her husband. Eric. That's his name. Back is her friend with the braid. Claire. Back is Jake. Her son, gone now but home for the holidays, and home again as soon as he can be.

Lots of lights line this highway. Lots of trucks nudging her into slower lanes. Tired of the pulsing noise of vehicles and the noise in her own head, she pulls off and goes into a shop with a neon coffee cup in front of it. When the server brings her cup, there's no money to pay for it. There's also no purse.

She puts her head on the table and begins to sob.

'Ma'am.' The server raises her voice. 'You can't be doing this. You're going to disturb our customers.'

'I am a customer.' She doesn't know how to say more. Then she reaches into the pocket of her jacket for a tissue and grabs her phone. Lifting it into the server's worried face, she says, 'I am a customer.'

Then she sees the text from Claire. *Tessa, please let me know you're OK. I'll find you wherever you are.*

She calls her back.

'Where are you?' Claire's voice is as calm and even as always.

She shoves the phone at the server and say, 'You tell her.'

Tessa's face heats as she waits for Claire to find her. She's not sure how she did this to herself when all she wanted was to get on a bus and go home. But she didn't go home. She went to hell.

The server returns, all smiles, carrying a cup of hot chocolate. Tessa can smell it through the melting marshmallows on top.

'On the house.' The young woman smiles and pats her shoulder. 'It must be awful to lose your purse. You sit right here and I'll keep my eye out for your friend.'

'Thank you,' Tessa says.

Did she lose her purse or just forget it? Maybe she dropped it in the parking lot. She sips the chocolate through the sweet froth on top and knows she has to go outside to look for it. Even with the rain, she needs to go out there. She takes another sip and glances through the window at the parking lot. There's her rental car, all right. Her purse might even be inside it. Then Tessa sees something else, a shimmering light above the car, an outline of a woman, a girl.

She stifles a scream. The shape of the woman blurs but Tessa can make out her features and the outline of her ice-blue dress. Then she hears laughter and sees the kids in the parking lot lifting glow-stick bracelets, laughing as their lights seem to bend and flow.

She lets out a sigh and reaches for the cup again. It was only the lights she saw. Only the lights.

FOURTEEN

Claire

'Claire, help.'

Claire pressed the phone to her ear. 'We got disconnected before, Tessa, but I can hear you now. Tell me where you are.'

She was surprised how calm her voice sounded, but it was the only way she could calm Tessa, the only way they could find her.

'Outside in the parking lot,' Tessa said. 'I saw something here, lights. I thought it was a woman. Please find me.'

'We will,' she told her. Sitting stiffly in the seat beside her, Eric reminded her of the way he appeared in television interviews, jaw set, speech clipped. He had covered this San Joaquin Valley highway in little more than an hour. But he wasn't in control. He only looked that way.

He glanced at her. 'I hope I didn't scare you. My driving, I mean.'

'I'm already scared,' she said.

He reached over and patted her arm again. 'Me too. At least we know where she is.'

'Yes, as long as she stays there.' She shivered.

Eric turned on the heater. 'She will stay there. She trusts you.'

Claire started to object and then thought about what he had said. 'She's done a lot for me too, changed my life really.' She sighed and collapsed against the car seat, rubbing her arms as the heater warmed them. 'I hate this, Eric. We're speaking of her as if she's dead.'

'Not true.' He pulled off the main road into a narrow street. 'We are reminding each other how important it is to save her.'

'But save her from what?'

'Whatever has her ending up in front of her mother's house when she's supposed to be coming home from work.'

'What do you think that is?' Claire asked him.

'Part of it's the way she's always been. I guess you could call it childlike.' At the stoplight, his expression softened and she could feel the sadness behind his smile. 'Being around her makes everyone feel younger, more joyful. At least, that's how it's been for me.'

'Me too.' She glanced out the window at the black, rain-wet streets and the small-town shops and partially deserted restaurants that looked like something out of an old painting. 'Maybe whatever is going on isn't a big deal.'

'Maybe a physical exam would help, as we discussed,' he said. 'But I am not subjecting her to a litany of psychological testing.'

She turned in the seat. 'Why not? If she needs it, I mean.'

'I told you about her father. Her mother has mental health issues, not to mention drug and alcohol addictions that, thank goodness, Tessa does not. She's terrified of being like her parents, though.'

'But she's not like them,' Claire said. 'What if a simple test showed that she had some kind of chemical imbalance that could be regulated?'

The light of the street cast shadows across his face, high-lighting wrinkles she had never before noticed. 'What if it showed it couldn't be regulated?'

'Wouldn't you want to know that too?'

'Not this early in the game. If that were the case, what would it matter? Either way, Tess and I are forever.'

Claire imagined Danny in a similar situation. He would never have stuck with her through anything this uncertain and potentially devastating.

'So what do we do when we find her?' she asked him.

'We get her home and we keep her safe.' He rubbed his forehead with his right hand as if trying to relieve a head-ache, but she knew that nothing was going to lessen the pressure of what they were facing. 'You might be right about her keeping the job,' he said. 'Can you take care of that for her?'

'I think so,' Claire said. 'As long as nothing else happens.'

'Nothing else?' He gave her an easy grin but his fingers

tightened around the steering wheel. 'Like Tessa disappearing and showing up an hour-and-a-half away?'

She met his gaze. 'No one is going to know that.'

'You won't tell anyone?'

'Of course not.'

He pulled onto a dark street running parallel to the freeway. At the stop sign, he looked over at her. 'Not even Al?'

'I don't talk to him much,' she shot back. Then, sensing his disbelief, she added, 'I have talked to him but we are not seeing each other, if that's what you're asking.'

'It's not, but thank you for telling me that.' He slowed the car as the lights of the fast-food places began to blur ahead of them. 'We're getting close, aren't we?'

'Very close.' She glanced down at her phone. 'It should be on the right side of the street.'

As she spoke, Claire looked out of the window and saw Tessa standing at the curb, waving frantically.

'There she is,' Eric said. 'I told you she'd wait.'

They both got out of the car and she rushed to them. Then she stopped as though not sure how to begin.

'I don't know what happened. I lost my purse.'

'How did you get here?' Claire asked her.

'I have a rental car.' She pointed to a sedan in the lot.

'Why don't you take it, Claire?' Eric said. 'Tess and I can follow you back.'

Tessa gave her a wide-eyed look as if begging her not to leave her alone with Eric just yet.

'All right.' Claire started toward the car. 'But I'll need Tessa to show me how to get there.'

'Of course.' Although his tone was careful, Claire noticed how he had not stopped scrutinizing Tessa. 'Do you know where you got the car?' he asked her in a gentle voice.

'I think so,' Tessa told him.

'Do you have whatever agreement you signed when you rented it?'

She bobbed her head. 'On the seat. I remember I put it on the seat.'

'That's good. You and Claire will be able to find the place, and I'll follow you.'

'I want to go home.'

'Well, then,' he said. 'Let's get you there.'

Tessa

Once Eric walks back to the car and she and Claire head over to the rental, Tessa finally feels safe. Claire won't judge her. Claire never does, at least not anymore. Sometimes she is too much the scientist to understand things, though. Sometimes, especially lately, she insists on medical help that Claire might need more than she does. Tessa watches as Claire studies the thin yellow paper from the rental car place and then gets behind the wheel.

'I'll drive,' she says, and Tessa is relieved.

She could navigate through this fog-splotched darkness if she had to, but she's glad to be sitting here in the safety of a vehicle with a driver who knows where she is going. Before they get this car turned in, she will share what she saw with Claire. There's something else she wants to share with her too, but she can't quite remember what.

She leans her head against the cold doorframe and tries to think.

'Want me to turn on the heat?' Claire asks.

'I'm fine.' The road signs look familiar. The houses along the street remind her of something she would rather forget. That's what the past does to you. It lures you in, and then the most innocent memory can multiply into others that, if you aren't careful, can break your heart.

'We'll get through this.'

Tears spring to Tessa's eyes. 'Are you sure?'

Claire reaches for her hand. 'Yes. You'll keep your job. Rosemary overacted, and she doesn't deserve to know that her outburst upset you this much.'

So it was Rosemary's fault. Maybe it really was. Rosemary and her ugly words. There's something wrong with her. Blaming it on her feels right. Tessa can go back home, back to work, back to being . . . what?

Claire pulls onto the narrow street leading to the bus station and the rental car office where Tessa took it out.

'Next time you decide to visit your mom, though, let me know, all right?'

'That's what was so weird.' Tessa waits until Claire parks the car. 'I didn't know I was going. I just got on a bus and kind of fell asleep.'

'I shouldn't have left you at the office.' Sometimes Claire likes to blame herself, and this is one of those times. 'I'm sorry.'

'We agreed to leave sorry behind,' she says. 'Maybe I needed to come here, to see her and remind myself why she's dead to me.'

'Next time, tell me.'

'There won't be a next time.'

'Before you go anywhere, I mean. Eric was worried.' Her voice softens, and Tessa knows she's trying not to sound bossy. 'So was I.'

'It won't happen again,' she says. Her leg brushes something and she leans down. 'My purse,' she tells Claire. 'I didn't lose it after all.'

She fishes around and takes out a nail file. Something about it makes her uncomfortable and she shoves it back into her purse.

Claire pulls off to the rental place, and Tessa glances behind them to see Eric's headlights following them.

Claire slows the car but doesn't quite stop. 'You are going to be safe now.'

'Yes, I am.' She bites her lip and knows she can't tell Claire that she might have seen the girl again. She can't share that with her now. 'I just want everything to go away.'

'Are you up to coming back to work tomorrow?' Claire asks. 'Because if you aren't, I can get you a little time off.'

'No time off, please.' She presses her palms together and realizes that they are sweating. 'I would go crazy if I had to stay in that house all day.' Then she realizes what she's just said and can't help smiling. 'I mean I would go crazy for real if I couldn't go to work.'

'Rosemary's being a real jerk,' Claire says. 'We're going to have to be careful.'

Translated: *You're* going to have to be careful, Tessa thinks.

'I'll be extra careful with the snakes.'

Claire squirms, and Tessa remembers how much she hates them.

'Maybe we can cut down the number of school visits for a while.'

'I'm fine to do the schools.' She squeezes Claire's shoulder. 'I hit a rough spot, that's all. With Rosemary scrutinizing me and then finding that woman's body with you, I overreacted.'

Claire nods. 'Is that what you're going to tell Eric?'

Until then, Tessa hasn't realized that's exactly what she is doing, creating a story to tell Eric.

'If he gets preoccupied worrying about me and loses the Sudbury case, that poor woman will be sentenced to prison, maybe worse.'

Eric stops the car a few feet behind them, and she can see the shadowed shape of him behind the wheel. 'Going to my mom's brought everything into perspective and I'm all right now. That's what I'm going to tell him.'

She glances over at Claire, wanting to say more but not knowing where to start, as Eric gets out of the car and walks toward them.

FIFTEEN

Claire

Claire sensed that Tessa had wanted to talk for longer the night before, but she didn't dare press her after all Tessa had been through. Instead, Claire would keep her word to Eric and try to make sure Tessa didn't get into more trouble at work. That morning, she changed her plans so that she could accompany Tessa on a school visit. That would probably appease Rosemary for a time.

The teal jacket Tessa had given her last year had always been too bright for her, but it was both light and warm enough for the changeable weather, so she put it on anyway. Tessa seemed convinced that she was going to be all right. Claire would go along with that, but if she wanted to protect her from Rosemary, she would need to watch her closely.

When she arrived at the greenhouse complex, she saw Rosemary's car in the parking lot and groaned. Not a good sign.

Claire straightened her shoulders and headed inside. If this were about Tessa, it was going to be a short conversation. She stepped into the lab room and spotted Rosemary behind the planting table, a wooden crate in front of her. Dressed in a cashmere cape and tall boots, she was clearly heading for a meeting and not for a day in the trenches. That was the good news.

'Good morning,' she said. 'I brought some other supplies that you left behind.'

'Thanks,' Claire replied, and waited.

'Oh, and I'm setting up a temporary office in the west greenhouse.' She pointed. 'I thought it would be a good idea to stay on-site for a while.'

'You don't like it in the college administration office?' Claire asked.

'For now, this is best. I can do my work here as easily as there.'

'Whatever you prefer.' Claire kept her tone civil.

'And we all need the same keys.'

'We all have the same keys,' Claire said.

'Not here. We need to be able to get into each other's offices whenever we need to. We can't be as lax as we have been. You'll have new keys on Monday.'

'Fine,' Claire said.

'Then I'll be going. I'm on my way to a meeting.' She glanced at the clock. 'Where's Tessa?'

'At a school visit.'

'Alone?' She cocked her head as if daring Claire to defy her.

'I'll be joining her shortly.' She forced herself to unclench her fists. 'Anything else?'

'Not really.' She started for the door and then stopped. 'There is one thing. Rather strange actually. Have you heard about Al Paden?'

'What about him?' Claire knew Rosemary was setting her up but she could still feel herself flush.

'He tried to coerce Bobby Glover's son into saying he had stolen Al's German Luger.'

'That's ridiculous,' she said. 'Glover already reimbursed him for the money he took, generously from what I understand.'

'As I said, it is rather strange.' Rosemary reached for the door. 'Why would Al try to make anyone confess to stealing his gun?'

'I don't know.' Claire gripped the edge of the table.

'Knowing what a hothead Glover Senior is, and with Eric for a friend, I'm sure he'll be pressing charges. Al and Bobby Junior actually got into some kind of fistfight.'

'How do you know all this?' Claire asked.

'A friend at the sheriff's department.' She glanced at the clock again and frowned. 'You would be surprised how many friends I have in this town.'

'I'm sure you're very well connected,' Claire said. 'Was Al hurt?'

'Not badly, from what I understand, but he's in trouble.

I wouldn't be surprised if he is just trying to cover up how his gun ended up in that car. Got to run now. Have a good day.'

The door swung closed behind her and Claire realized that she could barely swallow. She grabbed her coffee cup, filled it from the water cooler and tried to make sense of what Rosemary had said. Bobby Glover's son was one of several college kids who had burglarized a few small businesses, taking cash and anything else they could grab. It was a prank, Glover had insisted when the kids were arrested, and he had offered to make restitution for anything Bobby Junior took. In the case of Al, it was about a thousand dollars from the petty cash drawer. But it might have been his Luger as well. If Rosemary were telling the truth, he was in trouble. But that was a big if. Claire needed to find out for herself.

She sent Tessa a text, telling her she'd be late, and then she drove to Al's shop. Closed. Although the air still carried the chill of early morning, the sun had already come out and the sky was clear. Cupping her hand over the glass door, she peered into the front office. Unopened envelopes lay scattered across the hardwood floor beneath the mail slot. Al wasn't here today and hadn't been here yesterday either.

The loft he had purchased after he and Natalia divorced was only five minutes away. It wouldn't hurt to drive by there as well. As Claire drove, she reminded herself that Rosemary was close friends with Natalia and she had lied about Al before, saying he had cheated on Natalia while they were still married. Claire knew better. Maybe this wasn't as bad as Rosemary had suggested.

Located in the downtown's mural district, the lofts were lined up on a short street scattered with round, bolted-down metal patio tables. Large windows were bordered by narrow balconies shaped to resemble industrial catwalks. Al's shutters were open a crack and Claire rang the bell, knowing he would be able to see her if he were inside. She heard movement and the knob turned. Al stood just behind the security screen wearing faded jeans and a gray shirt the color of the slate wall behind him. The gash on his face looked fresh. Claire stifled a gasp.

'I heard what happened,' she said. 'Rosemary's version, at least.'

'I don't mean to be rude,' he told her, 'but I'm pretty busy right now. I'll give you a call later.'

He started to close the door but she put out her hand to stop it. 'Please, Al. I want to know what happened.'

'I'm on my way somewhere.'

'I won't stay long.' She forced a smile and made herself look directly at him. 'If I try to, you can throw me out.'

The door opened. He let her inside and walked to the open kitchen along the south wall. 'OK, can I get you some coffee?'

'I'm on my way somewhere too.' As she stood in the doorway, she was overwhelmed by the simplicity of the place, its walls covered with his large black-and-white nature photographs.

Although he admired the color work of contemporary western photographers, Al had always argued that black and white, light and shadow, made a stronger statement in a photograph. In their many conversations over the years, Claire had been certain she knew him. Now, she didn't know what to believe.

He came back carrying a white ceramic espresso cup by its metal handle and motioned with it toward the photo she was studying. 'That's a new one.'

A cluster of bare, snow-covered trees gleamed in moonlight, their intertwined branches making them look like ghostly creatures, their arms raised in an intricate dance.

'It's stunning.'

'I took that right outside Yosemite,' he said. 'Early this winter.'

He walked over to the tile counter and she followed, realizing that her jacket was the only color in this entire room. Not counting the wound on his cheek, that is.

'Have you seen a doctor?' she asked.

'No.' He ran his finger over it. 'I don't think I'm going to need stiches. That bastard was too quick for me.'

'Rosemary said it was a fistfight.'

'And Rosemary also said that I was cheating on Natalia before she left me. Another lie.'

Claire laughed. 'I had the same thought.'

Al placed his hands on the tile and turned to her. 'I didn't start it, only hit back. All I did was ask if he stole my grandfather's gun when he and his buddies broke in here. What did Rosemary say about that?'

'That you tried to coerce him into saying he stole the Luger.' Claire wasn't going to lie to him. 'That you're in trouble.'

'That last part might be true.' He moved his barstool around so that he could face her. 'I don't know what's going on, but someone is trying to make it look as if I put that gun in the car. And maybe that I had something to do with the woman's body.'

'Is that why you contacted Bobby Junior?' she asked.

'Of course it's why. Bobby Senior had already reimbursed me for the money his kid took but I never thought to check for the gun. Now, Bobby Junior's saying he didn't even break in here at all.'

'Why would he lie?'

'Either he's covering for someone or he's involved in something bigger.' He got up and walked to the white upholstered bench beneath a high rectangular window. A suitcase lay open on the bench. 'Either way, I don't need the hassle.'

'You're not leaving?'

'That's exactly what I'm doing.' Al closed the suitcase and faced her. 'I'm going to head over to the coast for a while, take some photographs and get out of the line of fire.'

'You can't.' She got up and went to where he stood. 'That will only put you *in* the line of fire.'

'Not if they don't know where to look for me.' He touched the mark on his cheek and grimaced. 'You know me as well as anyone. This is not who I am.'

'That's another reason you have to stay,' she said. 'So that you can prove you're telling the truth.'

'Why don't you come with me?' He said it the way he had asked her if she wanted some coffee.

'You know I can't do that.'

'You could visit.' He glanced over at the suitcase again and then back at her, squinting in the early morning sunlight.

'We're both divorced now, Claire. There's no reason we can't spend time together.'

He had to know she couldn't do that. Yet this was the same Al who had been her friend. She had liked him once and maybe loved him.

'There *are* reasons,' she said. 'I can't leave here until we find out what all this means, and I wish you wouldn't either.'

'Do you believe me?'

'I know you,' she said. 'I'm not sure how your gun got in that car, but you've never lied to me.'

'Thank you.' He moved closer, and for a moment she thought he was going to reach out for her. 'If you change your mind,' he said, 'I'll be in Cambria.'

She felt herself smile. 'For the record, a guy who's trying to disappear probably shouldn't reveal his destination.'

'You're the only one who knows it,' he said, and then his smile disappeared. 'Because you're the only one I trust.'

Tessa had kept her promise. Her school presentation was flawless and, as Claire watched her last one, she was impressed.

Tessa pointed at the screen in front of the classroom. The words *San Joaquin River* were superimposed over an aerial photograph of it.

'Does anyone know how to pronounce this?' Tessa asked the class. They laughed and pointed at a little boy in one of the middle rows.

'It's my name,' he said. 'The J sounds like a W.'

'And do you know how long the river is, Joaquin?' Tessa asked.

'Long,' he said, and everyone laughed.

'He's right,' Tessa told them. 'It's the longest river in Central California, 366 miles. Isn't it cool that it runs through our valley? We can see it anytime we want to.'

Even though Claire knew the material and had taught most of it to Tessa, she could never speak in public that way. She could never encourage questions and laughter, never respond with the kind of spontaneity that Tessa did. It was difficult to believe this was the same Tessa who had boarded a bus the day before and disappeared.

She could tell that Tessa was enjoying the attention from the young students. Occasionally she would glance at Claire as if to say, 'You see? I'm doing fine.' And Claire would smile and nod.

Yet her mind kept returning to Al. Although she knew that he was serious about leaving town, she didn't know if he were serious about asking her to go with him. At one time, she would not have even considered it. And now? He said he hadn't done anything wrong and she believed him. Cambria was only a couple of hours away. No, that was crazy. She needed to focus on her job. That's what a scientist did. Focus. Pay attention to detail. Isolate emotions.

By the time Tessa finished her afternoon presentations it was almost three o'clock. Claire walked with her to their cars.

'You were great,' she said. 'Better than ever.'

'I could do this in my sleep.' Tessa loaded the snake crates and computer into the back seat of the car and closed the door. 'I really do feel past whatever came over me yesterday. Thanks for standing by me.'

'That's a given,' she said. 'Once we finish up at the greenhouse, want to grab an early dinner?'

Tessa glanced away as she did when she didn't want to share something with Claire. 'I don't know if I can.'

'Eric?' she asked.

'Oh, no. He won't be home until later.' She looked down at her hands and rubbed her thumb against each cuticle.

'You have other plans?'

'Just some work I wanted to get done.'

'Not meeting with anyone?'

'Nope.' She leaned against the car door. 'You know what? Never mind. After all the drama we've been going through I'd actually enjoy a little downtime. Let's go get something to eat.'

When they returned to the greenhouse complex, Rosemary was not around but the crate she had left on the lab table was still there. Tessa and Claire decided to walk over to the university's farmers' market. The previous year, they had eaten there several times before shopping. Their conversation had been spontaneous then, unguarded.

Smoke from the tri-tip steaks and corn roasting on a barbecue pit outside drifted into the sky. Inside, they picked up their food and found a table in front of a window. Tessa sat down and motioned at the new construction outside.

'That's what got me in trouble yesterday,' she said. 'Somehow I got over there, wandering around, and the next thing I knew, I was at the bus stop.'

Her phone dinged. Tessa took it out of her purse, sent a text and turned back to Claire.

'Do you know why you wanted to get on the bus?' Claire asked. 'Did you see someone you recognized?'

'I just wanted to go home.' Her phone dinged again and she made a face. 'Once I got on the bus, wherever home was seemed to change and I ended up in that hellhole. But I'm fine now. I meant what I told you. I haven't felt this calm in a long time.' She picked up a piece of corn on the cob. 'And I'm not quitting my job.'

'I'm glad,' Claire said. 'You're good at it.'

'Eric thinks it's too stressful.'

'He's just trying to protect you.'

Tessa's phone rang again. 'Shut up,' she said to it and glared at her purse.

'What's wrong?' Claire asked her.

'Everything's fine. I told you.' She picked up a paper napkin and wiped her fingers.

'Who's trying to get in touch with you?' Claire said.

'I don't know.' She turned off her phone.

'Why not check? It might be Eric.'

'It's not.' Tessa shrugged. 'Timothy was worried because he couldn't reach me last night.'

'Timothy? If he's that worried, you should let him know you're all right.'

'I did.' She pushed her plate away. 'But he sent a text earlier and asked me to meet him at the river behind my house. He does that sometimes.'

'Do you think that's a good idea?'

'He's harmless, and he's scared to talk to most of the staff.'

'Talk about what?' she asked.

'Anything he's not sure of. Rosemary treats him even worse

than she does me, always acting like he's stupid or that he's screwed up something important.'

'She's not even his boss,' Claire said. 'But she could cause trouble for both of you if you keep meeting with him secretly.'

'We've always hung out together.'

'True. With Wally, Al, other people and me,' Claire said. 'But not alone at night. If she decides you're not acting in a professional manner, it would be just like her to complain to the board.'

'Screw the board. Most of them are Eric's friends anyway.'

'She might even go to Eric,' Claire told her.

'I don't meet him very often.' She rocked back in her chair, as if uncertain what she was going to say next.

'Let's go over together,' Claire said.

Tessa shifted in her seat and looked out the window. 'He may not even be there.'

'You could text him.'

'He might not come if you're there.' But he might. If Timothy was talking to Tessa, he might talk to Claire, too.

'He trusts me, doesn't he? He told me about seeing the girl on the river.'

Tessa pushed back her chair. 'You're right. But he doesn't know anything that's going to help Al.'

'That's not why . . .' Claire stopped the lie before she finished it. 'Al got in a fight with Bobby Glover's son and now the kid is saying he didn't break into Al's office at all.'

'Meaning?'

'That Bobby Junior claims he didn't steal the Luger.'

'Timothy saw it the same time we did. He doesn't know how it got in the car.'

'But maybe he saw something else.'

Tessa reached for her phone. 'OK. Even if he doesn't show up, we can walk through the old office. I'm not sure all my stuff got moved.' She sent a text and looked up at Claire. 'But I still think Al should fight his own battles.'

'He's doing the best he can.'

'Eric doesn't trust him.'

'What are you talking about?'

'I can just tell,' Tessa said. 'Every time he doesn't want me to know what he's thinking, he gets this kind of set expression on his face. That's what he does every time I mention Al.'

'That doesn't mean he necessarily distrusts him, Tess.'

'He's said some things too.'

'Like what?'

'I don't remember, but you've got to admit Al destroyed your marriage.'

This angered Claire more than it should have. 'No one outside the marriage destroys it,' she said. 'I destroyed my own marriage. Danny and I. We're the only ones responsible for that.'

Tessa started to respond but instead pressed her lips together.

They sat there a few minutes longer with their coffee until it became clear that Timothy wasn't going to reply to Tessa's message. She glanced outside again, as if looking for him.

'It's going to be dark soon.'

'We have time,' Claire said.

Timothy didn't show up, and so they went to their old office. No one had dusted or vacuumed, but the electricity was still connected. Once the maintenance crew got around to it, all of this stuff would go – unwanted furniture, paper files that were now digital, personal items that no longer mattered.

Claire pointed at the neatly printed notes to Maintenance on the door and on some of the boxes. 'Rosemary's been here.' She read from the one on the closest box. '*Please take extra care with this and deliver first. Ms Boudreaux.*'

'Nothing in there but a bunch of old files she didn't want to haul herself,' Tessa said. 'I got most of mine. Want me to help with yours?'

They collected some files Claire wanted to keep for backup, and after two trips they were able to get everything in the car. The air was cold but still, with no hint of a breeze. The trees were beginning to darken into shadows.

'I don't think Timothy or anyone else is out here,' Claire said.

'No, but the air feels good, doesn't it?'

'Why do you meet down here with Timothy?' Claire asked her.

'Because he needs someone he can trust.' She kept walking. 'And because he makes me feel safe.'

'What about Eric?'

She shook her head. 'Until he saves Gloria Sudbury, I can't bother him about anything.'

'But he loves you, Tessa. He drove like a mad man to find you yesterday.'

'He also barely sleeps at night. Every time I wake up, he's staring at the ceiling.'

They walked back inside to Tessa's desk, which Rosemary had labeled with Tessa's name and her new location.

'Look.' Tessa lifted a partially burned beeswax candle off the old metal typewriter table she had used as a shelf. 'Jake gave me that. I knew something was missing when we moved.'

Beside the table was another box Rosemary had labeled, *Trash.*

'She doesn't have any right to throw my stuff away.' Tessa bent down. 'Look at this. She threw out my whole file on our presentation plan for next year. She's probably going to claim I lost it.'

'We have all that online,' Claire told her.

'There's nothing wrong with having a paper backup. I mean, how much room does it take for one file?'

She sucked in her breath and stared into the box.

'What's wrong?' Claire asked.

Without answering, Tessa put down the file and pulled something out of the box – pieces of a torn photograph. Slowly, Tessa moved them together on the table and Claire saw that it was a younger, happier photograph of Eric and Tessa, ripped apart.

Her eyes filled with tears. 'Oh my God. Why?' she asked. 'Why would Rosemary destroy my anniversary photo?'

'I don't know,' Claire told her. 'But this is one thing you definitely do need to discuss with Eric.'

SIXTEEN

Tessa

Eric is on the phone when Tessa walks inside. He's still wearing his jacket, so she knows he must have just gotten home. The wrappings from a fast-food hamburger sit on the counter. The smell of it permeates the kitchen.

'I'll talk to you later,' he says into the phone and ends the call. He comes over, kisses her and says, 'You're home late.'

'You're home early,' she tells him.

'I was thinking it would be nice to spend the evening together. I was too hungry to wait for dinner, though. Today was an emotional drain.'

'I'll make some coffee.'

'I'd rather have wine.' He motions to the counter. 'You sit down and I'll get us both a glass. How was your day?'

'Eric . . .' She stands partway into the kitchen still holding her purse. 'How well do you know Rosemary?'

He puts the wine bottle on the bar and says, 'What do you mean?'

'She tore up our anniversary photo at the old office.'

'What? Are you sure?' His voice takes on that soft tone he used when he picked her up after she went to her mother's house.

'Of course I'm sure. She put the pieces in a box she labeled trash for the maintenance people to get rid of. Claire saw it, too.'

'That doesn't make any sense.' He pours their glasses and motions to her to join him. She crosses the room and sits on a stool beside him. He puts his arm around her. 'We've never worked together, and other than those charity events Bobby Glover put on, we've never socialized.'

'So, you don't think she's attracted to you?'

He laughs. 'Certainly not. But something's not right. She must have torn up the photo to upset you.'

'No.' She toys with her wine glass and looks up at him. His eyes are bloodshot, his face drawn. 'She didn't know Claire and I were stopping by. If we hadn't, I probably wouldn't have found it.'

'I don't know.' He shakes his head. 'Maybe you should just confront her and ask why.'

He stifles a yawn, and Tessa thinks she should have waited to bring this up.

'Maybe,' she says.

He has to make some calls and heads upstairs. Tessa considers listening in, but she's tired. Instead, she takes the pieces of the photograph out of her purse and puts them together again. The edges are jagged as if they have been ripped in anger. It makes no sense. She hasn't done anything to Rosemary – nothing she can remember.

She loses track of time, and now she wonders how long she has been standing out here on the balcony staring into the night.

'Are you there?' she says, but she knows the woman on the river never answers.

The French doors behind her open and Tessa catches her breath. It's Eric. He might have heard her and think she's talking to herself. She doesn't know what she will say if he has. But no, he's smiling, looking down and shaking his head.

'Barefoot again, Tess? When are you going to learn?'

Barefoot? He's right. No wonder she can't feel her feet.

'Come on.' He picks her up and carries her into the kitchen. It smells like hamburgers.

Tessa wants to ask why, but something tells her that she should know. So instead she says, 'Where are you taking me?'

And Eric says, 'To bed.'

Claire

That morning, on the way to work, Claire tried to call Al but each attempt only went to his voicemail. Cambria, she thought. Maybe she ought to just drive there. Instead, she sent him a text. *Give me a call when you can.* She felt better when they were in touch. His help at the pancake breakfast had calmed her, even when everything was falling apart. He had a point, too. They were both single now.

The greenhouse complex at the university was far calmer than the river offices had been. She and Tessa settled down to work and pretended to ignore Rosemary's comings and goings.

Claire tried to analyze what they were doing. It wasn't denial, more like putting off the inevitable. Until the woman's body was identified, until the horror of that discovery began making sense, she and Tessa went through their days, their school meetings and their planting sessions as they always had. They even continued their walks along the river path on their lunch breaks. It was only ten minutes away from their new office. They had protested for this right, after all.

They left their office, reached the golf course and turned around before crossing the boundary that separated the public road from Winston's property. As they stood there, catching their breath and looking up the hill at the backyards overlooking the river, Claire breathed in the clean air and wondered how so much in her life could have changed so drastically. Her marriage. Her friendship with Tessa. Her trust in Al.

'Did you talk to Eric about your anniversary picture?' Claire asked.

Tessa nodded. 'I wish I hadn't. He was exhausted and didn't know anything about it. All it did was give him another reason for wanting me to quit my job.'

'Well, don't do that.'

When Tessa left to change for a presentation, Claire went over to Rosemary's office. Timothy was just leaving and Rosemary was standing in the middle of a room of boxes.

She looked up, as if surprised to see Claire standing there.

'I was just getting ready to leave,' she said. 'Did you need something?'

'Actually, I wanted to ask you something.'

'Good.' Rosemary walked outside, locked the door and leaned against it. 'I've been wanting to discuss Tessa with you anyway.'

'I think we already had that conversation.'

'Not really,' Rosemary said. 'You can't continue to cover for her.'

'Just a minute,' Claire told her. 'Before you even start, you need to explain something to me.'

'I don't have to explain anything to you.' Her cheeks flushed. 'And don't speak to me in that tone. It's unprofessional, and frankly, you don't pull it off that well.'

'Tessa and I went to the old office the other night.'

Rosemary's face was deep red now. 'Good. I'm glad I'm not the only one doing all the work.'

'We found all of your notes to Maintenance.'

'Most people would thank me for being so organized,' Rosemary said. 'This is a major move and we should all do our part, even if it's not listed on our job description.'

'We are doing our part.' Claire fought to keep her voice even. 'That's why we were there.'

'I've got to go.' Rosemary started toward the parking lot. 'If you have anything else to discuss, you can tell me on the way.'

Claire matched her steps. 'We went through the trash box by Tessa's table,' she said.

'And? Let me guess. You're upset I threw away a file even though all of the information is stored electronically now?'

'Tessa wasn't happy about that,' Claire said as they approached the parking lot. 'But she was more upset when she saw the photo of Eric and her.'

Rosemary's posture stiffened. 'And what was I supposed to do with it? Leave it in the file cabinet?'

'Why did you destroy it?' Claire asked.

'I didn't.' Rosemary took her keys out of her purse and met Claire's eyes. 'Tessa tore up that photo herself.'

'That's a lie.'

'No, it's not. I saw her doing it right before we started moving. When she realized I was watching her, she hid the pieces in the file cabinet.' She pulled her sunglasses out of her purse. 'Apparently she has forgotten what she did.'

'No,' Claire said. 'You're just trying to set her up again.'

'She's doing a fine job of that herself.' Rosemary put on the sunglasses. 'Seems to me there's a lot you don't know about your friend.'

Claire watched her walk away toward the parking lot, the
mountains in the distance, the day crystal clear and cold.
She wanted to call out to Rosemary, to demand answers,
but she didn't know where to start. She had nothing to say.

SEVENTEEN

Claire

C laire woke realizing she couldn't believe Rosemary. As troubling and forgetful as Tessa was, and as much as Claire believed she needed a medical evaluation, it was obvious that she was genuinely shocked to find the pieces of the photograph. Claire decided not to tell her what Rosemary had said.

The following day, Tessa arrived at the office the same time Claire did.

'Didn't you have a school visit?' Claire stopped at the door and noticed that Tessa's eyes were brighter than usual. She looked the way she used to, when they would have their adventures visiting various nurseries in the area to purchase unusual native plants for their greenhouses.

'The teacher changed it to Wednesday.' Tessa looked down at her boots, which were immaculately polished.

'You look great,' Claire said. 'Are you feeling better?'

'Better than better. Finally, something good is happening.'

'What do you mean?'

Tessa walked in behind her and stopped at the lab table. 'Have you ever seen Eric in action?'

Claire laughed. 'Other than the way he handled my divorce, you mean?'

'Oh, that's right.' She nodded. 'Winston is selling the golf course.'

Claire couldn't help wondering if the discovery of the dead woman had also influenced his decision to sell. If he really had decided. If this were not wishful thinking on Tessa's part.

'Who's buying it?' she asked.

'I couldn't hear that part.' She turned her back to Claire and began making coffee.

'So you overheard a phone call?'

'Just cleaning the guest bedroom.' She mumbled the answer as if struggling with the lie she was creating. 'I know it's true, though. Eight o'clock this morning.'

As the smell of coffee filled the room, she joined Claire at the lab table.

'It's already ten minutes past that,' Claire said.

Tessa shoved one hand in the pocket of her jacket and took a swallow from her mug. 'Then it's already happening.'

They drank their coffee in silence. 'You don't believe me,' Tessa said. 'Do you?'

'I'm not sure what you mean,' Claire told her. 'That Eric found a buyer for the golf course? Why would he do that, and how would he have time to put pressure on Winston to sell while he's working on the Sudbury case?'

'He said it came together effortlessly. Said it would be good for the community.' Tessa clasped both hands around her mug. 'That's all I know.'

'All right,' Claire said. 'Good, I guess. Let's get to work.'

'Not yet.' Tessa walked around the table. 'I am not making this up. I know something is happening at eight this morning.'

'It's already eight-fifteen,' Claire said.

'Well, let's go over there then. I'll prove it to you.'

'You don't have to prove anything to me.'

'I do.' She climbed off her wooden stool. 'I need to prove it to me.'

'All right.' Claire poured her coffee in the sink, went to Tessa and put her arm around her, thinking about that woman's body in the water and how Tessa had broken down.

'Do you really want to go back there?' she asked.

She nodded. 'I'll be OK. I would have been when we went to the office if I hadn't found that photo.'

'You know it isn't going to be easy for either of us.'

'I don't care,' Tessa said. 'I want you to know I'm not making this up. Winston is selling the golf course and Eric is involved.'

Tessa was already heading out of the room, her immaculate boots clicking on the floor.

Claire caught up to her and let the hood of her jacket slide onto her shoulders.

They took Claire's car to their old office, parked it and walked the short distance to the driving range.

Tessa stopped and turned toward the river. Claire did the same. 'Do you really want to go inside?' she asked.

Tessa nodded. 'I need to.'

'Are you sure we should interrupt?' she asked.

'Eric won't mind.'

'But he doesn't know you overheard his call.'

'Oh, that's right.' Tessa stopped for a moment. 'It will be OK, though.'

'But . . .' Claire had to get her to clarify, to keep from embarrassing Eric if he were really there. 'Help me understand this for a minute. Is Eric helping a client buy the golf course?'

'That would make sense.'

'But you aren't certain?'

'Only that I heard him say Winston will roll over for this deal. That they can get it cheap.'

'Winston's a jerk, but what reason does he have for taking a low price?'

'He doesn't want to deal with more protests,' Tessa said as if reciting it. 'He doesn't want sheriff's department cars parked out on the bluffs.'

'Not to mention . . .' Claire couldn't finish the rest of the sentence. She still saw the shape of the body in her mind.

'Winston will fold. That's how Eric put it.'

She and Tessa stood overlooking the drop to the river on their right.

Tessa was so lost in this idea of Winston selling the course that she seemed to believe it was the answer to everything that had gone wrong – the broken car, the gun, and the body in the water.

'I'm sure. Better yet, so is Eric. Are you OK with going in there?'

'If you are.' Claire pulled her jacket closer.

She still wasn't sure Eric would want them walking into the middle of a negotiation that must be tense. But she couldn't think of any other argument, so they walked down the path. Outside the clubhouse, they both stopped. To the right, the white motorhome the river conservancy kept for supplies and an occasional security guard looked as dingy as always. Beside it, Timothy's truck was parked, steam still rising from it like fog in the early morning.

They stood outside the small gray building and Tessa started walking again. 'Come on, Claire.'

Claire followed her toward the door just as Timothy came up the walk.

'Hey, there.' He reached in his pocket and pulled out a handful of keys. 'Winston asked me to meet him here to change the locks.' He rattled the keys in his hands. 'Looks like he's leaving.'

'You see,' Tessa said.

The three of them walked to the clubhouse. Claire stopped just inside the door. The smell of coffee filled the room. Wearing a gray suit, Eric stood over the two men seated at one of the round tables inside the kitchen. Bobby Glover, who wore his tight pastel-blue shirt like an athlete past his prime, crossed his arms over his chest, and Winston scrawled his signature on a pile of legal-looking papers in front of him.

'So, it's done,' Eric said. Then he looked up and gave them a frozen smile. 'Tess, Claire. What a nice surprise.' He looked anything but happy to see them.

Tessa paused and then moved closer to Claire. 'I just wanted to show her.'

Winston jerked himself to his feet. 'You win,' he told Eric. Then he turned to Tessa and Claire, his tanned cheeks now crimson. 'You win too. May your victory give you women everything you deserve.'

With that, he headed out of the door. It swung slowly behind him and cool air filled the room.

Timothy jumped and dropped the keys.

'It's OK,' Claire told him.

He scrambled to pick them up. 'Guess I'll change the locks then, if that's all right.'

'It's fine,' Eric said. 'Congratulations, Bobby. This is an excellent deal. Having the ladies show up wasn't in the plan, but it was a nice reminder of the opposition he'd be dealing with if he stayed. He doesn't want any part of this place. Tess, honey, we did it.'

Tessa seemed stiff and unnatural. Probably thinking about the body again, Claire guessed. And probably thinking about how small this victory was in light of all that had happened.

Eric noticed it too and moved around the table until he was beside her. 'Tess?'

'I'm fine.' She glanced over at Timothy on her other side. 'We're going to fix the locks, right? So no one can get in here again?'

'Right,' Timothy said.

The way she spoke to him and the way he answered seemed too close and in some way inappropriate.

The smile left Eric's lips. 'Well, I'm happy to hear that,' he said.

Tessa's grin tightened. She put her purse over her shoulder, slipped her hand in it and then stopped. Slowly, she lifted her right hand out of her purse and pulled out a small red box. She frowned at it and placed it on the table where the men had been sitting.

The black print on the box read: *9MM LUGER. Made in Switzerland.*

'What's that?' Eric asked. He couldn't miss the way Timothy and Tessa looked at each other and at the box. 'Where did you get this, Tess?'

'I . . .' She cocked her head and glanced down as if she had never seen it before. 'I'm not sure.'

'Well, I am sure of one thing.' Eric snatched up the box. Bullets spilled from its crumbling cardboard. Eric tapped the side of the flimsy container. 'These are Luger bullets. Aren't they, Claire?'

Her mouth went dry. 'I don't know,' she said.

'I'm sorry.' Eric squeezed her arm in a way he must have felt would support her. 'I have to turn these in. You understand, don't you?'

Claire tried to nod, tried to smile, tried to do anything but break down in tears.

'Sure,' she said, and as she did, she glanced at Timothy, still holding his keys, and at Tessa, with her wide-eyed expression of innocence. In that moment, Claire knew that both of them were lying, if only by omission.

By the looks Timothy and Tessa exchanged, Claire knew this wasn't the first time either one of them had seen the bullets. It wasn't the first time she had seen a box like that either. Al had already admitted that one of his was missing when he showed her the empty gun box. She needed to talk to him, to let him know that Eric was going to turn over the box. Yes, she realized, she was going to take a chance and try to protect Al even though he hadn't even replied to her text. Maybe phone reception was poor where he was. Or maybe he didn't care.

After Timothy left the building, Eric insisted on driving Tessa to their new office and Claire drove alone. Tessa was sitting, hands folded on her desk, when Claire walked in close to eleven.

She stood up and said, 'I'm going to clean the pond.'

Before Claire thought to tell her that could wait, Tessa headed out of the side door and down the path. Claire could follow her or go through the lab and into the first of the two greenhouses on this side. Tessa clearly needed space. One wrong word and she would retreat into herself again. She had been doing that more and more frequently, acting exuberant at some times and vague and disconnected at others.

9MM LUGER. It couldn't be a coincidence. Claire had to convince Timothy to tell her where he had found that box of bullets.

Claire sent him a text. *How long will you be at the river?*
Had to go home. Took afternoon off. Back later.

Claire checked the records for his address, but when she drove there she realized it was a postal store with rented mail slots. When she returned to the greenhouses, the intermittent wind had worn itself out, leaving the surface of the pond a calm, deep green. Tessa stood with her back to Claire, expertly skimming the pine needles and yellow leaves. Focused on her task, she cut through the debris, lifted and slammed her long net against the side of the trash barrel.

'Need any help?'

Tessa shifted the net to her left hand and turned around. 'I've got it under control.'

'I need to get in touch with Timothy.'

'He's around.' She moved to the other side of the pond and Claire followed her. 'Actually, he's the one who should be doing this job. We're too busy with the move and all.'

'Tessa,' she began.

'He actually likes cleaning the pond. Says it relaxes him.'

'Was he the one who gave you the bullets?'

The screech of birds soared over them.

'Seagulls.' Tessa turned to the window. 'They're heading east. That means a storm's coming.'

'When did Timothy give you the bullets?' Claire asked. 'How long have you had them?'

'I don't remember.' She stopped, and the net dangled from her hand into the still water. 'Don't you have something else to do, Claire?'

'No. Not until we have this conversation.'

'That's going to have to wait.' She lifted her foot. 'Look at that. The water's soaked through my boots. I'm going to go dry out. Since you're so willing to help, why don't you finish the job?'

She shoved the handle of the net into Claire's hands and hurried up the path toward their office. Claire stood there, then finally put down the net and followed.

By the time she stepped inside, Tessa sat barefoot on the edge of her desk. Her tall boots and burgundy socks were spread out on the floor between her and the space heater.

Claire shut the door behind her. Tessa turned, her eyes wide and unfocused. She glanced around the room as if looking for a way to escape.

'It's all right,' Claire said, keeping her tone even. 'I just need to know where Timothy lives.'

'With his sister and Jack. Her name's Ginger.'

'I know that, but where?'

'I'm not sure. Somewhere past Dickerson Avenue, out near Ripperdan.' She lifted her dirty hands, frowning at them as if uncertain how they got that way. 'Why do you care?'

'We've been friends too long to play games, Tessa. I'm guessing he's the one who gave you those bullets.'

'He's just trying to help.'

'So am I,' Claire said. 'And I'm on your side. Remember

that. I could just go to the main office and look up his address. I could go online.'

'No, don't do that. Please.' She jumped down from the desk and stood close to the space heater. 'If Rosemary starts asking questions, there will be no end to it.'

Claire moved slowly toward her until Tessa backed up and slid onto the stool again. They were eye to eye.

'I'd rather you just tell me where I can find him.'

Tessa stared down at her bare feet. 'Why can't you wait until work tomorrow?'

'Because I need to know about those bullets now.'

Her head shot up. 'He's afraid he'll get blamed. He always gets blamed.'

'That's why I've got to talk to him. Did you see the look on Eric's face when he saw the bullets? You know he'll tie them to Timothy, don't you? And the sheriff's department will tie him to you.'

'Eric would never hurt me,' she said.

'Of course not. But he'd never withhold evidence either. How many times have we heard him say that?'

She pulled her hair away from her face and lifted her chin. 'Who are you really trying to protect?'

'You, for starters.' Claire gripped the corner of the metal desk. 'Anyone can see that the box has been in the water. The bullets probably came from that car and the gun that was in it.'

'Timothy knows that.' She rubbed her hands together as if trying to warm them. 'He was just afraid to turn them in.'

'Well, Eric will take care of that,' Claire said. 'And what's Timothy going to do then?'

'Just tell the truth, I guess.'

'You said he always gets blamed. Don't you think he'd like to talk unofficially?'

'Are you saying that you're a neutral party? That you don't have a personal interest in this?'

'That's it.' Claire crossed the room in a few steps. 'I'm going to find him with or without your help.' She stepped outside and fought the urge to slam the door.

'Wait,' Tessa called from behind her.

She turned and waited.

'The beagle rescue,' Tessa said in a broken voice. 'Timothy's sister runs it and he rents the flag house in the back.'

'How do I find it?' she asked.

'Just go straight west on Herndon. When the road narrows, you're almost there.'

Tessa

Tessa's socks are dry enough. As she pulls them over her feet, she thinks they look like the color of blood. Bad things will happen now, because of her, because of those bullets. She slides off the desk and tries to think of something happy, but nothing is happy. The slight jolt of the sliding glass door in the lab room tells her that Claire has returned, but when she gets up from the desk and goes out, it's Timothy standing there, just inside, holding the wad of keys.

Tessa gasps and steps back.

'I waited until she left.' He chews his bottom lip the way he does when he isn't certain what to say next.

'That was a smart move,' she says. 'Claire's looking for you.'

'That's why I didn't go back to the river. I knew she'd try to find me.'

'She's going to your house right now,' she tells him.

Timothy pales. 'How does she know where I live? No one knows where I live, not even you.'

And because the intensity of his gaze frightens her, Tessa turns away, toward the window, and says, 'I think she checked the records.'

'The records don't know either.' He moves closer to her and forces her to look at him. 'I pick up my check at work. I have my mail sent to a postal store.'

'You did tell me about the beagle rescue,' she says. 'And the flag house.'

His eyes remind her of something . . . someone she doesn't want to remember.

'And you told Claire that?'

She nods. 'I didn't know it was a secret.'

'Everything we talk about is a secret.' He shoves his hands in his pockets as if trying to look strong. 'Did you tell her where you got the bullets?'

'Kind of.'

'And what are you going to tell your husband?' Although he doesn't move, Tessa feels herself draw back. 'What are you going to tell him?'

'That I don't remember.' She looks up into his eyes, and smiles. 'There's not much he can say to that.'

Wind against the glass doors shatters the silence and they both turn. Timothy pulls his watch cap down around his ears.

'I'm in trouble,' he says.

'No, you're not. It's just the wind.'

He doesn't seem to hear her. 'I found the car. I found the gun and I found the bullets. They're going to blame everything, including the dead woman, on me.'

'We don't even know that her death was a crime,' she says.

'Oh, there's a crime, all right.' Wind rattles the glass again and Timothy turns in the direction of it. 'I need to stop Claire before she goes out there.'

'You can't.' Tessa reaches out for his sleeve, but he is already heading for the door. 'She was going straight there when she left.'

'Then I'll catch up with her,' he says. 'You wait.'

'Wait where?' Tessa asks. But he has left the way he came, through the glass door, hurrying toward his truck.

Tessa wants to run after him, but even if she could catch up before he drives away, she doesn't have the strength to stop him. She wants to warn Claire that he is following her, but she knows Timothy is no real danger to Claire or anyone. Probably she should just go home, but she can't bear the thought of Eric's questions.

Through the door, she can see the path to the pond, a job she started but didn't finish. Her socks are warm against her feet and she doesn't want to repeat that mistake. The yapping of the seagulls covers the sky again. Tessa closes the door behind her and retraces her earlier path, one careful step at a time.

EIGHTEEN

Claire

Claire arrived after three o'clock. After forty-some minutes of wide-lane street, the road narrowed until it was only two tapered lanes with houses on the left side and the deep drop to the water on the right. Although she wasn't as familiar with this west side of the river, Claire wasn't surprised to see white cattle egrets poised over the alfalfa fields looking for insects. She hadn't taken the time to ask Tessa what the flag house was. Still, once she found the beagle rescue she would find Timothy.

The tough beauty of the blue-gray water and the dying reeds surprised her. Contrasting sharply, tract houses set back from the road seemed unfriendly or at least withdrawn. A couple in sweats and heavy jackets walking small dogs ignored her as she passed. Then she saw the van and the smiling cartoon dog faces on its side. Beagle Rescue Service.

Parked at the end of a long gravel driveway, it sat beside a sign that read: *Beagle Rescue. Drop-offs will be taken straight to the SPCA.* Beneath that was a phone number. Claire made a U-turn and realized that the property held a second house that had been hidden behind the first. Its slanting tin roof glinted in the sun. Red, white, blue. Someone had painted an American flag on it. The flag house.

She got out of the car and tried to decide if she should approach the front door or follow the driveway back to Timothy's house. Just then, Jack, walking a small black-and-white dog with a tan-coloured spot covering one side of its face, came out of the flag house and started toward her. He took his time, the little dog trying to urge him along. A pastel-blue shirt tucked into a pair of jeans emphasized Jack's eyes and his ruddy complexion matched his weather-beaten hands. Once he'd noticed her, his smile came easily.

'Good afternoon.' His voice was unadulterated Boston. 'Are you the lady who called for this little guy? I was just getting ready to walk him.'

'Jack,' she said, 'it's me, Claire.'

'Oh. Of course.' His manner became formal as effortlessly as if he had flipped a switch. 'I didn't recognize you with your hair down.' He transferred the leash to his left hand and held out his right. 'This is Argos. What's Timmy done this time?'

'He hasn't done anything,' she said. 'I just need to talk to him.'

'So do I.' Argos jerked at his leash and Jack shouted, 'Sit.' Argos obeyed and then tried to bounce ahead.

'This one is Type A for sure.' Jack grinned at the dog and started down the drive. 'You're welcome to come along with us, but I've got to get Argos some exercise before his new owner comes for him.'

'Is Timothy in his house?' She gestured back at the strange little barn-like structure. 'It's kind of important.'

He stepped onto the road and started toward the narrow end of the street where it appeared to be a dead end.

'Important to me, too. Timmy still owes me back rent.' He stopped and glanced over at her. In the chilly afternoon light, his pale blue eyes widened and he shook his head as if trying to find the right words. 'He's had some bad breaks.'

'Like what?' she asked.

'I suspect you have an idea, or you wouldn't be out here.'

'I don't know what you're talking about,' she said. 'I just need to ask him something.'

'I'll bet.' He snapped the automatic leash and the dog ran ahead. Jack's pace increased. 'I'm just saying that whatever he's done this time, well, I hope you go easy on him.'

'Don't bait me.' Heat rose to her cheeks. 'If you need to tell me something about your brother-in-law, please do. If not, just tell me where to find him.'

'Ma'am,' he said. 'Claire. I have no idea where he is at the moment. Timmy . . . he's, well . . .' He tapped a finger against his head.

'He does an excellent job for us,' Claire said. 'I'm not here because of anything he did.'

Clouds covered the sky, dimming the sunlight. Tessa had been right about the gulls. Claire could already smell the coming rain.

'He's been in trouble before, you know,' he said. 'Poor kid can't seem to tell the truth. Old Wally always covered for him, but when he passed I knew it was just a matter of time.'

'Jack,' she said, and he stopped the way the dog did when he gave it a command. 'Timothy isn't in any kind of trouble. I just need to speak to him about something and I don't want to do it at work, where others can hear us.'

'I don't know how he does it but the kid does have a talent for making pretty ladies want to help him.' He chuckled and wiped the back of his hand across his forehead. 'If that's why you're here, good luck. Believe me, Timmy needs all the help he can get.'

'But he lives here, doesn't he?' she asked.

'Not for some time.' He reached down and petted the dog. 'Come on, Argos.' He began to jog and Claire stayed behind, watching him move away from her into the hazy light.

After Claire left Jack, she drove to their old office on the river bluffs, but Timothy wasn't there either. The rain had arrived, a soft, constant downpour. No point in trying to look for Timothy now. She might as well call him again and then go to the university office to make sure Tessa had really locked up.

She took out her phone and, as she glanced down at it, a text appeared on the screen. *I'm back. At your office. Need to see you.*

Al. Finally.

She turned east, heading for the university. At the first stoplight, she replied. *On my way.*

As she pulled into the back parking lot, she heard the faraway sound of a marching band. Although the music building was on the other side of the campus, the athletic complex was at the other end of the street. She saw the familiar white car and caught her breath. Al got out and walked over to her. Rain plastered his hair against his scalp but he didn't seem to notice. The cut on his face had scabbed over. Claire unlocked the door and he got in.

'I'm so glad you came back,' she said.

He took off his glasses and dried them with the bottom of his jacket. 'I got your text.'

'You didn't write back.'

'I was distracted.' His jaw tightened. 'The sheriff contacted me today,' he said.

'About the bullets, you mean?'

'Of course about the bullets. Someone turned them into the sheriff, and if a crime really was committed with that gun, if that's what killed the woman they found, I'll be the one they arrest.'

A crime had been committed; that was clear to everyone now. And his gun was probably involved. That didn't mean he was, though.

'Timothy found them,' she said. 'I've been driving all over the west side today looking for him.'

He turned to face her in the seat, his wet hair almost black. 'I don't believe Timothy turned them over to the sheriff.'

'I didn't say he did.'

'But he gave them to someone who did.'

'Yes.' Then she realized what he was suggesting. 'You don't think I turned them in, do you? Tessa had them in her purse, and when she pulled them out and Eric saw what she had, he took them.'

'Why didn't you tell me?'

'I meant to,' she said, 'but I thought you'd get back to me, and I've had my hands full here.'

'I would have preferred hearing the news from you instead of the sheriff,' he said.

'Then you might have replied to my text.' Claire could no longer maintain her calm facade.

He glanced away from her, through the windshield, and she got a better look at the cut on his face. 'You aren't the one who turned them in?'

'Seriously, Al, why would I turn in the bullets?'

'Because of us, maybe?' He glanced back at her. 'Because you think I'm the one who made that call to Danny?'

'Even if you were the one,' she said, 'even if you did call Danny, I would never try to harm you. We were friends before anything else. Remember?'

'I remember, all right.' Still holding his glasses, he turned to her. 'What really happened, Claire? First the gun and now the bullets. I know you're not doing this to me, but who is?'

'I don't know if anyone is doing it *to* you.'

'Someone is,' he said. 'Eric?'

'In the case of the bullets, maybe. But he really did have an obligation to turn them in.'

'I get that,' he told her. 'But you've turned into a different woman.'

'Of course I have.' And he had turned into a different man, one who was capable of fighting with Bobby Glover's son, of running away instead of standing up for himself. 'What happened with us, between us . . . it destroyed my marriage,' she said. 'It ruined my relationship with my daughter. So, yes, I'm different, but I would never try to incriminate you. And I know you didn't have anything to do with whatever happened to that woman.'

'Yet you thought I'd stoop low enough to call Danny.'

'That's what he implied.'

'You believed him.' He reached for the door handle. 'What would I have to gain by making that call to him?'

'I don't know,' she said. 'But who else would know?'

'There were fifty-plus people downstairs at the party that night.'

'Not that late.' She felt herself flush. 'Everyone had drifted out onto the mall before you and I went upstairs.'

He shook his head slowly, his eyes fixed on hers. 'I would have gained nothing by making that call. But by convincing you of it, Danny wins everything.'

'How?'

'By keeping you away from me. By putting doubts in your mind.'

The truth hit her. Maybe that was Danny's revenge, a way to make her distrust and avoid Al.

'I gave him more credit than that,' she said.

'I know.'

Silence filled the car. Then, from far away, they could hear the mismatched sounds of the marching band, all drums and belching horns.

'That explains why I could never really believe you would do that,' she said. 'You're too decent.'

'So are you.' He turned toward her, his fingers still around the door handle. 'When the sheriff started asking me about the bullets that showed up in the office of the driving range, I went a little nuts.'

'They only showed up there because Tessa forgot she had them,' Claire said. 'Timothy found them on the bluffs. That's all I know.'

'We should have talked sooner,' he said.

'I texted you!'

'And I guess I was angry and confused.' He ran his fingers through his damp hair. 'If I could go back and change what happened with us that night, I would.'

'Me too.' Then she knew he deserved better than platitudes. 'Most of it, at least.'

His lips relaxed into a smile. 'Most of it.'

This is what had really ruined her marriage, not the anonymous phone call, but what she had experienced with Al, what she still felt – the anticipation, the attraction, the recklessness. That's what she had missed until that night. Even long before then, it was what she had craved.

The band music boomed louder, cymbals and tambourines. In full uniform, young men and women marched along the street in front of the car, almost drowning out the conversation with their noise. So much for privacy.

'Is this a game night?' she asked as she felt herself break into a smile.

'I have no idea.' Al shrugged and then smiled back. He must have been hoping for a private conversation as well.

'I have to go,' she told him and hesitated, considering whether they should continue their talk elsewhere. 'But what do you think we should do to prove the gun and the bullets were taken from your office?'

'I don't know.' He watched the kids march away. 'I guess we need to figure out who did take them.'

'Do you think it was Bobby Glover's son?' she asked.

'Well, Bobby Junior made it pretty clear that his denial stands.' He touched the cut on his face. 'If he's telling the truth, someone else had to break in there. And if he's lying, he's trying to cover up something worse than the burglary.'

'Maybe he's lying because he's afraid.'

'Or because he's guilty.'

'I know Bobby Junior,' she said. 'We've talked at parties at Eric and Tessa's. Actually, he's pretty outgoing. I've never found him to hold back much.'

Al shook his head and reached for the door handle again. 'He's not going to admit breaking in to you any more than he did to me.'

'You're probably right,' she told him. 'And I really should go. I still need to check the greenhouses.'

'This late?'

'With all the kids out here tonight, I probably ought to.' She wasn't going to tell him that sometimes Tessa forgot to lock up.

'I'll go with you.' He got out of the car before she could object.

They walked up the path, and the soft light made his eyes look the way he must have as a child, large and questioning.

'I always wondered why you do this kind of work.'

'Why I do what?' she asked.

'Planting trees, pulling out invasive plants. Why do you do it when you know the odds are against you?'

'Why are you trying to save downtown?'

'That's different,' he said. 'I believe I *can* save downtown – a little piece of it anyway.'

'And I believe I can save the environment – a little piece of it anyway.'

'And I can't imagine myself doing anything else.'

'Neither can I.'

He put his arm around her and she forced herself to turn away. They couldn't touch, couldn't kiss. That would only complicate what was already a mess. The inside lights were on, the door unlocked.

'Great,' she said. 'Someone forgot to lock up.'

'Tessa?'

'Not necessarily. She, Rosemary, Timothy and I all have keys. Timothy is supposed to do the final check but he's not out here full-time. The last one to leave should have done it, but we do leave it open for night classes.'

She opened the door and he followed her inside.

'It's a lot older than your river location but also much bigger.' He walked from the lab room into the office with her and Tessa's desks. 'My sunset photo,' he called back to her. 'I didn't know you'd kept it.'

'I've always loved it,' she said. 'Besides, that was one of the few times you've ever photographed in color.'

'Not even a black-and-white photographer can resist an occasional sunset.' He walked back and stood in the doorway between the two rooms, looking at her, and Claire knew they'd better leave right then.

Something brushed her leg. She glanced down, saw Colby the snake and stifled a scream. Al spotted him at the same time.

'Don't move,' he said. 'I'll get him.'

Colby brushed her leg again, and Claire forced herself to stand perfectly still. 'Stay where you are,' she said, knowing her tone was almost robotic. 'Best to stay calm so as not to startle him.'

'Claire, what do we do?'

'He's harmless,' she said. *Harmless*, she told herself, and broke out into a sweat. The problem was in her head. 'Come slowly over here, though. I'll need you to pick up his back end. We can't startle him. First, though, check the cage.'

He moved to it a step at a time. 'The black one's half in and half out.'

'Roscoe,' she said as Colby's skin slid over her bare ankle and she tried to repress a shudder. 'He's harmless. Please put him all the way inside, lock the door and then come help me over here.'

She tried to shut down her emotions as Al made his way carefully to the cage.

'When I approached, he went in on his own,' Al said, looking back at her. Then he walked over to where she stood. 'I can do this.' He glanced down at Colby. 'I know you'd rather not be anywhere close to these guys.'

'I'm fine,' she lied. 'Wet a paper towel for me at the sink, please, so I can clean my hands.'

'Why can't I just pick him up?' Al asked.

'Because you don't know how, because I do, and because without clean hands, especially if he is hungry, we could smell like dinner.'

Al reached over to the lab sink, wet and soaped up a paper towel, then handed it to her. She wiped her hands and then hoped she could go through with the rest of it. Slowly, she leaned down and spoke softly to Colby the way she had heard Tessa do.

'Hey, big guy. You ready to go back in your house tonight?' His skin tensed against her hands and she shivered. 'You'll be fine.' She looked up at Al. 'Wash your hands, too, and then help me.'

Trying to ignore her crawling flesh, she picked up Colby and began to lift him. 'You take the tail,' she told Al. 'Keep it at this height.'

He gently lifted Colby so that their hands were at the same level.

'Back to your house, Colby,' she said. 'Back to your house.'

As if balancing a small, tense hammock between them, they moved in a slow dance toward the cage. Claire reached out, unlocked and opened the door, and Al helped her guide the snake through it. Then, as Colby's tail cleared the door, Claire closed and locked it firmly.

Trying to stop the tears burning her eyes, she went to the deep stainless-steel sink and let the water stream over her hands, her wrists, her elbows. Al joined her and she clasped his fingers, pressing her face against his chest. He lifted his damp hands from the basin and put them against her cheeks. As water ran down her neck and onto her jacket, he held her tightly.

NINETEEN

Tessa

Tessa sits on the bed, still wearing her jacket. She has taken off her socks, which turned out to be still wet. She tries to sink into the softness of the room, the luxurious duvet in blue and gray, off-center, one corner touching the hardwood floor as if in an advertisement, the other one bunched around her neck.

Something isn't right but she doesn't know what it is. Something about work, about the new office. Did she forget to lock the door again? She might have done something worse. Yes, that's what is bothering her. She betrayed Timothy at the meeting with Winston, Eric and Bobby Glover. She put those bullets on the table and now Timothy could be in trouble. She can't let that happen.

Eric steps inside, still wearing his suit. 'How's my girl?' he asks.

'Scared.'

'You're all right.' He comes over, sits next to her on the bed and lightly massages her neck. At one time Tessa would rise to his touch. Now, she tenses. 'Easy,' he says, his voice melodic. 'You're all right.'

'Did you give the bullets to the police?' she asks.

'The sheriff's department.' He says it almost pleasantly, as if discussing what they might have for dinner. 'You know I had to do that, and once you explain where you found them, you'll be fine.'

'Will I have to talk to them?'

'Them?'

'The sheriffs.'

'I'm not sure,' he says, 'but either way, you don't have anything to worry about. We don't own a German Luger, after all. Finding a clue doesn't make you culpable.'

'What if I don't remember?' She looks up into his eyes and sees only kindness, concern.

'I bet you'll remember,' he says.

Doesn't make you culpable. The words jam together in her head until they are one word, one sound.

The next morning, as soon as Eric heads for work, Tessa gets up, shivering in the early morning air. She won't tell him, can't tell him who gave her the bullets. But he is her husband. She can't lie to him, not forever. She needs to warn Timothy but she doesn't know where to find him.

I need to talk to you. She sends a text.

No answer. It's too early, almost six in the morning. She sends another text. *Meet me at the river by our old office. I'll bring coffee.*

That makes sense. Almost everyone is at the college office now. If he meets her early enough, no one will see them. And Timothy loves mochas. She'll bring him a big one.

Balancing a cup in each hand, she walks along the bluffs. Their old office, with its blinds up and partitions removed, looks like a hollowed-out building. She walks down toward the golf course and stands looking out at the river, trying to erase the image of what she and Claire found out there. Then she glances over at the broken-down white motorhome on the edge of the bluffs and sees that Timothy's pickup is parked beside it. The truck windows are frosted over. He must have been in the motorhome for a long time. She walks over and knocks on the door.

Slowly, it opens and Timothy stands there, buttoning his shirt and yawning.

'Are you living here?' she asks.

'Just for a while.' He motions her in and pulls a sweater on over his shirt.

The place is crowded with gardening tools and large jugs of chemicals. A tiny table holds his phone and an almost-empty jar of instant Folgers. And there's a chair with a blanket pulled over it.

'Oh, Timothy,' she says. 'What happened?'

'It's OK.' He grins as if living in this thing is normal. 'I'm glad you brought coffee.'

She glances down and sees the bulky gym bag he had that night by the river. It's full of clothes. 'But why are you here?'

His eyes grow wide and he looks at her the way he does when he's afraid to speak.

'No one knows where you are,' she says. 'Do they?'

'Jack, my brother-in-law, thought it was time for me to be on my own.' He takes the cup from her, clears the table and offers her the only chair. Then he sits on a large wooden stool. 'He's probably right. The flag house doesn't have any heat or AC.'

'Neither does this. Why'd you come here?'

'Kind of keeping an eye on the territory,' he says. 'That's how I seen the girl that night. Don't tell anybody where I am, though, OK?'

'OK.'

'Not even Claire.' She bites her lip as he adds, 'She doesn't like me.'

'Sure, she does.'

'Nope,' he says. 'She doesn't like me watching out for you.'

She's not sure that's true, but Timothy is so agitated that he has to hold his coffee with both hands. 'All right,' she tells him. 'Not even Claire.'

'I'm going to get blamed for everything,' he says. 'That woman's body – shit. I'm glad you ladies were the ones to spot her and not me.'

'The bullets.' She can barely speak. 'Eric turned them into the sheriff's office.'

'Have you told him where you got them?'

'No, but he says I might have to talk to the sheriff.'

'Just say you forgot.'

'I already did, but Eric can tell when I'm lying. I'm afraid he'll make me say.'

'You can't, Tessa. If you do . . .' He slices his finger across his throat. 'That will be it for me.'

'They already think there's something wrong.' Tessa struggles to find the right words. 'Something wrong with me, I mean.'

'There ain't nothing wrong with you.'

'But they're watching me. I hear Eric talking about me on the phone. Ever since I got on that bus, and they came to get me, I don't even trust Claire.'

'Me neither.' He pushes back his seat and it drags across the floor. 'Does she have a reason to make it look like I had something to do with that dead woman out there?' He points toward the view of the river through the side window.

'Al Paden,' she tells him. 'Those were his bullets and that was his gun.' Then Tessa realizes what she has just said. 'But Claire wouldn't lie. She wouldn't try to accuse you of anything just to protect Al.'

'She's been poking around,' he says. 'Even went out to my sister's, looking for me.' He tapped the phone on the table. 'Jack called, all pissed off.'

'She just wanted to talk to you about the bullets.'

'You told her?'

'She guessed.'

'Guessing isn't the same as knowing.' He's standing now, looking down at her. 'But she'll tell Paden, and if he has done something wrong we could both be in big trouble.'

Tessa starts to object, but then she realizes that Timothy is far from stupid.

'What can we do?'

'For one.' He walks over to a box on the counter by the river window. 'Protect ourselves. And two, don't go walking around this place at night.'

'Sometimes I have to,' she says. 'I can't stay away.'

'Try not to.' He reaches into the box. 'But if you do, you need some protection.'

He takes out a pistol, picks it up with both hands and brings it to the table, placing it in front of her.

She feels her breath suck in. 'What would I do with this?'

'Like I said, protect yourself.'

'But don't I have to register it?'

'I took it from Jack.' Timothy touches it the way he might pat a dog. 'Numbers have been filed off.'

She feels herself flush and puts her cool hands against her cheeks. 'Won't he want it back?'

'He don't know I took it.' He sits down beside her. 'Jack's not a bad guy, but he thinks I'm so stupid that I can't figure out he's selling firearms to anyone who wants them, and I don't just mean at his shop.'

'Illegally?' she asks, already guessing the answer.

'Can't tell you much about that.' He glances down at the gun again. 'Take it.'

'It might be dangerous out here,' she says. 'Are you sure you don't want to keep it for yourself?'

'It's all right.' He nods toward the box on the counter. 'I got another one.'

Claire

Claire and Al talked in bed that night. He told her about going to Austria for a photoshoot, meeting Natalia, a beautiful attorney, and falling in love with her. When her friend Rosemary Boudreaux said she could arrange US citizenship if they married, Al was surprised but willing.

'Natalia had everything I didn't,' he said. 'She was exotic, outgoing and articulate. She could walk into a room and everybody turned to look at her.'

'You never told me much about her.' Claire couldn't say more, not even in his bed.

'I couldn't.' He touched her cheek. 'But I should have waited.'

'Why didn't you?'

'Two reasons,' he said. 'The first one is that Natalia made me feel like the most desirable man in the world.'

'I can understand that,' she joked.

'The second reason.' He turned Claire's face so that they were looking at each other, their noses almost touching, his breath on her face. 'You were married. I thought if I got married, you and I could be the way we had always been.'

'Friends?' she asked, her voice shaking.

'Friends,' he told her. 'You know why, don't you?'

She nodded. 'I think so.'

'Because,' he said, 'we were always more than friends.'

Early the next morning, Claire fought waking up. In the chilly air under the skylight of Al's loft, the bed was not only warm, but safe. She didn't want to move.

On his back beside her, Al breathed evenly, one arm slung out from under the blanket. Although she had blamed the first time they were together on alcohol, she had no excuses now. But, as always, the timing was wrong. They should have waited, at least until Al was no longer a person of interest. If anyone from the sheriff's department came and discovered her here, it would look suspicious.

Claire, you're a cheater, a liar. Your whole life is a lie. That's what Danny had told her after he had gotten the call about Al and her.

A scientist who was afraid of snakes and who was rational only on the surface. A supposedly stable, married woman who had cheated on her husband and alienated her daughter. A woman who was unable to help her best friend and who had complicated her relationship with the man she cared about.

Danny might have been right about her after all.

Claire slid out of bed without disturbing Al and made her way down the spiral metal stairs. At the kitchen counter were the proofs of some photographs he had taken of a sunset over the river, a gleaming pink strip across a shadowed sky. Not quite color, he had joked, but a compromise.

She found a pen and left him a note beside the photo. '*Didn't want to wake you. Had to go to work.*' At 6:05 am? Why not?

She didn't say more. They could have that conversation, later and in person. Right now, she knew what she had to do. The drama department, across the campus from their greenhouses, was open early. After going home, showering and dressing, she headed there.

She had run into Bobby Junior on campus several times and he had always seemed happy to see her. Although he said he had compromised with his father and was studying to be an attorney, he spent a lot of time before and after classes hanging out with the drama majors. He was there that morning, as he had been almost every time she had seen him.

The dimly lit theater was empty except for him and two other students giving each other lines. He looked up, saw her and walked to the door where she stood.

'Hey, Doctor Barrett.' His eyes were large and blue like his father's and his hair sun-streaked. 'We're rehearsing *Waiting for Godot*. What do you think about Beckett?'

'I'm afraid I'm not very well versed on Irish playwrights,' she said.

'But Samuel Beckett was way more than a playwright.'

'I'm sure he was.' She gestured that he should keep his voice down. 'I didn't mean to interrupt your rehearsal.'

'No problem.' Now he sounded like the Bobby Junior she knew. 'We were ready to break anyway. What's up?'

'Would it be OK if we went outside?'

'I can take five minutes.' He glanced back at his friends and then at her. 'Is everything all right?'

'Yes, fine.' She started toward the door and stepped outside, grateful for the sunshine through the clouds. 'I just wanted to ask you about what happened at Al Paden's office.'

'Dad doesn't want me talking about that. Eric doesn't want me to, either.' His hand flew to his right eyebrow and Claire could see a raised surface there, even though he had tried to cover it with stage makeup. 'I've already gotten in enough trouble this year.'

'That's how you learn,' she told him. 'By doing crazy things.'

They walked down the ramp from the theater onto the sidewalk. He stopped, crossed his arms and looked at her.

'I'll bet you've never done anything crazy.'

'I have.'

Your whole life is a lie.

She could hear Danny's voice as Bobby squinted his disbelief.

'You didn't do it for the money, did you?' she said.

'I can't, Claire.' Bobby started back up the ramp and she followed him.

'So who are you in the play?' she asked. 'Vladimir or Estragon?'

That got his attention. He stopped. 'Don't know playwrights, huh? Actually, I'm the messenger boy, but he's a very important character.'

'He is,' she said. 'Why'd you do it, Bobby? Kicks?'

'The play?'

'You know what I mean.'

'A dare.' He gnawed his bottom lip. 'It wasn't the first one, but Al Paden is lying. We didn't go near his office.'

'Why not? You broke into the ones on either side of him.'

'Because of the woman.' He touched his eyebrow again. 'My dad is going to kill me.'

'I won't say anything.'

You're a cheater, a liar.

'I saw a woman in there a few nights before when we were planning which places to hit. The lights were off and she was going through the cash drawer. We didn't want to get blamed for whatever she was doing, so we skipped Paden's.'

'Does Al know that?' She barely recognized her own voice.

'I tried to tell him,' he said. 'But he called me a liar. I've got to go now, Doctor Barrett.' He turned and jogged up the ramp, toward the theater, leaving her standing there.

If he were telling the truth, that meant Al had withheld information from her. He had never mentioned that Bobby saw a woman in his office. Claire needed to go back to his place.

When she got to her car and checked her phone, she had a call and a text from Rosemary.

What's going on with Tessa? the text read. *She came in but said she had to go home.*

When Claire tried to call Tessa, there was no answer. As much as she wanted to talk to Al, Claire needed to check on her. After leaving the college, she drove to her house. Tessa met her at the door, holding a mug of tea.

'I didn't mean to worry you.'

'You didn't,' Claire lied.

'I went in today,' she said, 'but I was just too tired. I couldn't deal with Rosemary or any of it.'

'Deal with any of what?'

'Here's the latest.' Tessa put down her tea on the ebony entry table, picked up her phone and handed it to Claire. 'From Timothy.'

Sheriffs found the rest of the car. Looks like a train hit it. Blood inside. Lots.

'The car. Well, we knew they'd find the rest of it sooner or later.'

'I just want this to be over,' Tessa said.

'Maybe it will be today.' Claire took her arm. 'Come on. Let's get out there.'

TWENTY

Tessa

Tessa feels as if they are sailing.

Claire is focused on driving around to the west side of the river bluffs, down from Tessa's backyard, beside the overhead train tracks. It is the place where Tessa and Timothy meet sometimes when no one else is around, or at least when the ones who are around hide themselves.

'I don't even know why we're going out here,' Claire says. 'But we're part of it in a way. We found the body.'

She says something else Tessa can't hear. Her words blow out of the window into the early morning fog.

They pull into the cul-de-sac not far from the sheriff's department van. Tessa looks behind them and sees other cars stopping along the street.

Without speaking, she and Claire get out for a better look. Before them, something rests on the bank of the river where she and Timothy first talked. Rosemary rushes up.

'What is it?' she demands, pushing back her stiff black hair as if the wind could possibly damage it.

'The rest of the car.' She points. The sheriffs have pulled a large, lifeless metallic white vehicle from the river.

Claire sucks in her breath. Rosemary makes a similar noise, or maybe it is just the sound of crows overhead.

Tessa reaches for Claire's arm but Claire, like everyone, is gasping at the sight of twisted metal.

Tessa begins to tremble.

'Come on,' Claire says, but her voice is tight and Tessa knows she is thinking about Al and his gun. 'They will probably trace it now, and soon we'll know everything.'

Rosemary isn't moving in the wave of curiosity toward the wrecked car. She's walking – no, running – back to her own vehicle.

'Look.' Tessa points.

'I'll be right back,' Claire says, and takes off after Rosemary.

Claire

Claire caught up with Rosemary when she was almost at her car.

'Wait!' Claire shouted, trying to catch her breath.

'You have no right to question me and I don't have to stay here.' Rosemary fumbled in her shoulder bag, searching for keys.

'We aren't talking about rights.' Claire pressed her back against the driver's door. 'You've been trying to implicate Al in that woman's death from the start. Why run away now?'

'I'm not running.' Rosemary found her keys and yanked them from her purse. 'Get out of my way, Claire.'

'Not until you tell me what scared you back there.'

'What do you think scared me? A woman was murdered out here on our river.'

'We already knew that,' Claire said. 'You were happy to blame Al for it. What's changed?'

'Nothing.'

'No, something has. Do you recognize that car? Is there something in it that's going to prove Al is innocent?'

'He's not innocent. Now get away from me.'

'Not a chance,' Claire said. 'Not until you tell me the truth.'

Rosemary's eyes darted up and down, and Claire wondered if she was actually measuring their differences in height and weight. Claire had her beat with both.

'Forget about me,' Rosemary said. 'You can't make me stay here. Besides, you need to get in touch with your boyfriend before the sheriff does.'

Rosemary shoved Claire back, climbed into her car and drove away.

'What happened?'

Tessa joined her and they both watched Rosemary's car disappear around the corner. 'Where's she going?'

'I don't know.' Up close, Claire could see that Tessa's eyes were bright with tears. 'Are you all right?'

'I saw her again.' She pointed back at the river. 'This time she was laughing. Then I heard you shouting at Rosemary and she disappeared.'

'Who did you see, Tessa? The same woman you saw before?' Claire asked, keeping her voice calm.

'I think so.' Tears ran down her cheeks. 'What's wrong with me, Claire?'

'You just need rest. We've been through a lot. Come on, let me take you home.'

Claire stayed with her until she calmed down. Then she left a message for Eric, telling him that Tessa was home and upset. He called within the hour saying he couldn't get back until later.

'Please don't leave her,' he said. 'We can't take a chance after what happened before.'

He promised to return later that day, so Claire suggested to Tessa that they drive to the university. Tessa agreed reluctantly but seemed to brighten when they let themselves into their office and discovered that Rosemary was nowhere to be found. Eric met them in the late afternoon to take Tessa home.

'Sorry,' he said and joined them in the lab room. 'I was in court.'

Claire felt Tessa tense beside her. 'They found it,' she told him.

'I heard.' Eric joined them and put his arm around her. 'I talked to someone from the sheriff's department. It shouldn't be long now.'

'It brought everything back, Eric.'

'I understand.' He squeezed her shoulder. 'Tess, why don't you wait for me in the car? I left it unlocked.'

The moment she stepped outside, he turned to Claire. 'Thank you,' he said. 'After what happened in Wasco, I'm just afraid to leave her alone.'

'I understand.'

'I know you do, and I hope you also understand how grateful I am.' His voice caught and his eyes filled. 'I can't stand what's happening to her. Sometimes, it's almost too much for me.'

'For me, too.'

'It's as if she drifts a little farther every day and I'm having a harder and harder time of hanging onto her.'

'Sometimes she's better.' Claire realized she was almost whispering. 'I do think seeing a doctor might be a good idea. At least then you'll have a better idea of what your options are.'

The door opened and Tessa walked back into the room, eyes wide. 'Forgot my scarf,' she said and grabbed it from one of the stools. 'Are you ready to go, honey? I'm starving.'

'Sure.' He took her hand, said, 'Thanks again, Claire,' and they left.

Claire almost ran to her car.

The scent of downtown after a light sprinkle was the way Claire imagined the city smelling years ago, as if it had retained not just the old buildings but the aromas and the memories of the past as well. It reminded her of her grandfather, who had founded his trucking business down here and raised her mother, who had escaped the San Joaquin Valley and headed for the East Coast as soon as possible.

Although her parents believed that her job wasn't really science and that this agricultural community was beneath their family, it was the only place where Claire had ever felt connected to anything. She never felt closer to her grandfather than she did here on these streets where he had opened his first business – streets that had changed both so much and so little. Danny used to say that when the big quake eventually came, Downtown Fresno would collapse into itself. She liked to think that those old buildings would be the only ones left standing. But then, she realized, her work involved trying to understand and preserve the vulnerable past and Danny's involved trying to profit from the future.

From outside Al's office, she could see him, in cargo shorts and a T-shirt, bent over something on the counter. When she came through the door, she breathed in the smell of chemicals.

'I just printed out that photo you like.' He grinned, crossed the room and put his arms around her. 'You should have woken me up this morning.'

He started to kiss her but she stepped back.

'They found the rest of the car in the river today. They'll be able to trace it now.'

'They already have.' He hesitated and then said, 'It's Rosemary's.'

'Rosemary's? How do you know that? She's driven the same car as long as I've known her.'

'She rented it.' He walked over to the counter and pulled out a stool for her. 'Two guys from the sheriff's department were here this morning.'

'Why?'

'Because they think I killed that woman they found. They didn't put it like that but it's pretty obvious.'

'You need to talk to Rosemary,' she said. 'I need to talk to Rosemary.'

'She's disappeared. Not returning calls. Not at home. No one knows where she is.' He picked up a pencil and began to absently doodle on a pad.

'You should have seen her face when she saw what was left of that car. She knew they were going to connect it to her.' Claire was certain that was what had happened. 'She's somehow involved with the dead woman.' Her arms and legs felt numb and she slid onto the stool. Rosemary, she thought. Connected to the dead woman. 'Did the sheriff say anything about the body they found?'

'Nothing.'

'Have you thought about— I mean, only one woman is missing.' That's all she had been able to think about. 'Where's Natalia?'

'She's not missing,' he said. 'She's back home. Besides, Rosemary would never hurt her. They're best friends.'

'But where is she?'

'I have no idea,' he said, 'and even if I did, I wouldn't pursue it. She's the one who left me. Once she was a US citizen she couldn't wait to get out of our marriage.'

Natalia.

Claire shuddered, and yet she knew this was the only thing that made sense. 'That could be her body they found. We should have thought of it sooner.'

'No, Claire.' He shook his head. 'I don't believe it, especially not now with Rosemary racing away, too. If anything, they're probably meeting up somewhere where I can't find either one of them.'

'Why would you want to?' she asked.

He shrugged. 'Natalia might think I'd try to stalk her again or something. I'm way past that now.'

'You stalked her?'

He flushed and put down the pencil. 'I admit I was angry, shocked.'

'What did you do?'

'It doesn't matter.'

'It does if that's Natalia's body,' she said.

'You know I would never harm her, but I did follow her, OK? Lost it and banged on her front door. She threatened to call the police and I came to my senses.' He pressed his fingers into his temples as if the memories were causing physical pain. 'That was when we first broke up.'

'We need to find her,' she told him. 'Surely you know how to reach her family.'

'Except that they hate me. They didn't want her to marry an American. I told you that.'

'But now you have to contact them,' she said. 'If they tell you she never made it back to Austria, then we will know.'

He walked to the back door, opened it and winter wind blew through the screen. 'I'll call,' he said, 'but that asshole brother of hers probably won't answer when he realizes I'm the one calling.'

'At least try.'

'I will,' he said, 'I want to know the truth but I'm also in a lot of trouble here, trouble I didn't bring on myself. The last year has been hell. The divorce. Losing my friendship with you. And everything else.'

The cool breeze drifted from the back door to where she stood.

'Come here,' Al said, but she couldn't move. 'There's something else, isn't there? What is it?'

'I talked to Bobby Junior,' she said.

'Why would you talk to that little punk?'

'He told me he didn't break in here.'

'He's lying.'

'Is he, Al? Why didn't you tell me about the woman he saw in here?'

'Because that's a lie, too.'

'What's the truth then?'

'That he's lying for some reason. Bobby Senior and Eric are probably telling him what to say to lessen the charges against him.'

'Maybe he's not lying.' She joined him at the back door. 'Maybe Natalia took the money, Al. Maybe she took the bullets and the gun as well.'

He stood silently, his jaw clenched. Then he said, 'That sounds like something she would do, just to screw with my head if nothing else. But I know she went home. I would have heard from her family if she hadn't arrived.'

'Even though they hate you?'

He shook his head. 'Maybe not, but Rosemary would have heard.'

Rosemary was the key. She had to know what had happened to Natalia.

'I'm going to search her office,' Claire said.

'I'll go with you.'

'No,' she said quickly. And then added, 'If someone finds you there, it will look really bad.'

'I don't want you going there alone at night,' he said. 'Wait until morning.'

By morning, the sheriff's department might take possession of Rosemary's office and its contents. Claire didn't tell him that, though.

'Good idea,' she said. 'I suppose I should head home.'

He breathed in the air and took her hand. 'What does it smell like to you?' he asked.

Like hope, she thought. Like something important.

'I can't put a name to it,' she said. 'Some scientist I am.'

'It reminds me of that first night.' He pressed his lips to her hair. 'Come home with me.'

'I can't.'

He moved away from her and stared into the alley. 'OK, Claire,' he said. 'Call if you need anything.'

He was still standing there as she walked to the door.

Within forty minutes, Claire was inside Rosemary's office in the university greenhouse complex, her heart hammering against her chest. When Rosemary had insisted that they all have keys to each other's offices, Claire knew it was a move to enable Rosemary to spy on Tessa. Now, she was grateful that she could search for information without requesting entry from anyone.

The office was small with a metal desk, one chair and an empty bookcase. On the floor, three cartons were packed neatly to the top. Claire sat down on the carpet and began unpacking. Letters of commendation, awards, grin-and-grab photographs and official records filled the first. She started to open the second and then caught sight of some thin yellow papers she had overlooked in the first batch. Her fingers tingled. These looked like the ones Tessa had handed over the night she had gotten lost. Rental car forms.

As Claire reviewed them, she began to understand what had happened. The most recent payment on the mangled car was for this month. For some reason, Rosemary was still renting it, even though it had been demolished. The sheriff needed to see these. Claire gathered them up. As she did so, she noticed something else.

In the space requesting an alternate phone where she could be reached, Rosemary had filled in Danny's number.

At the River
November

Natalia drives along the road below the train tracks, and realizes that she won't miss this place with its sharp geographical divides and unsophisticated locals who believe a city block or two can define them. The entitled ones gravitate north to this part of town. The end of the city. It is their way of saying they have all they want. Others like Al head downtown, where it costs almost as much to look as if they don't care about material possessions.

Although they have parked here only six minutes at the most, darkness seems to have slammed down on them.

She has explained what she needs to, and now she waits for the reaction. When no reaction comes, she can't help adding, 'Actually, I'm doing you a favor.'

'*Cut the altruistic crap,*' *her passenger says.*

Anger, good. This is more like it. '*Only two people will know where I am or why. Well, three, counting you.*'

'*I have no interest in where you go as long as it's far away from here.*'

Just then, a truck pulls onto the road. It stops, and two young people get out. Holding hands, they run to the edge of the bluffs as if unaware how steep the drop is. They kiss, grab at each other's clothes and then glance over at the car.

'*So now we have an audience.*' *She drives farther up the road, past the kids, so that they are looking down at where they parked moments before.*

She hears movement, the unclicking of a door lock. '*You can take me back down there or I can walk. I really don't care.*'

'*You haven't heard a word, have you?*' *For a moment, she thinks of the gun under her seat, but this anger is momentary, gone as suddenly as it arrived. She lowers the windows and takes a deep breath.* '*I thought you'd care about why this is happening. I thought you would want to make it easier for all of us.*'

'*You said what you came here for. I'm leaving now.*'

'*But you can't,*' *she says.* '*You have to let go.*'

The passenger door swings open and the woman looks back at her. '*You poor, dumb bitch,*' *she says.*

TWENTY-ONE

Claire

C laire went through the other two boxes in Rosemary's office just to be sure she didn't miss anything else. The entire time, her heart raced and she kept trying to figure out Rosemary's connection to Danny. Of course they had met, but they had seemed only friendly in a professional sense. Somehow, they had become close enough that she had used his phone number as her alternate.

It was too late to pay Danny a visit tonight. That could wait. Right now, she needed to get this information to the sheriff.

'You shouldn't be doing that.'

Claire gasped and jerked to her feet. Timothy leaned against the closed door, his face set in a serious expression.

'I'm not doing anything.'

'I seen you in here. You can't take anything out.' He reached out his hand. 'Give them papers to me.'

'They're nothing,' she said. 'Just some contracts I needed.'

'Maybe so, maybe not.' He closed and opened his hand.

'Where's Rosemary?' she demanded.

'Beats me.' He moved closer to her. 'Claire, you've always treated me all right. Let's not change anything right now.'

'You're protecting Rosemary, aren't you?' She backed away from him and bumped into one of the boxes.

'No, I don't like her any more than you do.' He moved closer. 'My job is to keep watch on this place, and when I see someone this late at night trying to take something out, I got to stop them.'

'Don't you care what happens to Tessa?' she asked.

'Almost more than anything.' He continued to move toward her.

'What I just found in here can help Tessa,' she told him.

'It will help her understand what she thinks she saw on the river.'

'There ain't no one on the river, and never was.'

'There is to her.'

'That's just something in her head. I told her I seen the girl too and it calmed her down a little.'

'You never saw a woman out there?'

'I'm not crazy, Claire.'

'Neither is Tessa.'

'She's been slipping for a long time. That's why I'm staying out at our old site.'

'Staying where?' she asked, her thoughts conflicting. 'At our old office?'

'Tessa knows. That's enough.' He cleared his throat. 'Before Wally died, he asked me to look out for her, and I sure can't afford real estate in this part of town, so I'm just doing the best I can.'

'Why did Wally want you to look out for Tessa?' she asked.

'Because we were buddies, the three of us. Tessa is good people, and when Wally saw her fading, he knew you and that husband of hers wouldn't believe it.'

The wind rattled the trees outside and the office door shook.

Timothy reached into the pocket of his jacket and pulled out a gun.

'No.' Claire said. 'Put that away.'

'Sorry.' He put it down on Rosemary's desk. 'I thought someone was trying to break in.'

'It's just the wind.' She moved away from the desk, closer to him and to the door. 'Where did you get that?' She couldn't even say the word *gun*.

'No disrespect, but sometimes it's best not to ask too many questions.'

'Did Jack give it to you?'

'Did he *give* it?' He shook his head. 'No, he didn't, and that's the God's truth.'

'I need to leave now,' she said.

He shook his head. 'Can't let you do that. Not with them papers.'

'I understand.' She backed closer to the door as she talked.

'Would you be all right with letting me take just one of the papers?'

'Nope.' He smiled. 'Sorry.'

'What if I took a photo of one of the pages?'

He smiled again, his lips tighter this time. 'Not until I look at everything and make sure it don't hurt Tessa. If you're as good a friend as you claim to be, that should be fine, right?'

'Right.' Her voice came out in a rush. 'That would be fine, Timothy.'

'Good.' He wiggled his fingers at her again. 'I'd like those papers now.'

Claire reached into her purse and tried to separate one page from the rest of them. Then she crumbled the others in her hands and lifted them out.

'This is a mess.' She handed them to Timothy. 'I'm sorry they're so disorganized.'

'I don't care.' He glanced over at the gun and then back at her. 'I just need to look at them.'

'Of course.' She tried to breathe evenly. 'Look as long as you like, but I'm exhausted. Is it all right with you if I leave now?'

He seemed to think about it, and Claire wondered if she should run for the door. If she did, and if he grabbed that gun, he could kill her.

'Tell me.' He moved close to her, up to her face, until his eyes were a blur. 'Why should you get to leave here right now?'

'Because I love Tessa,' she said. 'Because I want to protect her just as much as you do.'

He glanced at the gun again and then back at her, and then he broke into the friendly smile she recognized.

'All right.' He stepped away from the door. 'Just don't tell her or anyone else about this conversation we had.'

'I won't,' she said, and backed out of the door before he could change his mind.

After taking the paper to the sheriff and going home, Claire couldn't sleep that night. Every time she tried to drift off, she kept seeing Timothy with that gun. She kept hearing Al admitting that he'd stalked Natalia. Danny was connected to all of this, too. At noon, she called him and asked him to meet her at his new home. He refused.

Although he had given her the address, this was the first time she would see for herself where he had decided to settle. The community, if it could be called that, had been a good idea in concept – a cloister of long, low houses set back from the river with landing strips instead of driveways and hangars next to their garages. Claire wasn't sure she would have been comfortable here, and not just because of the noise of takeoffs and landings. Along the winding street, wide driveways housed classic cars and an occasional motorcycle.

As she turned onto Doolittle Drive, she spotted the split-level, L-shaped home that had to be his.

He was climbing into his truck as she pulled up the wide driveway behind it.

'Wait,' she called through the window.

He stopped, got out and approached her, huffing. For a moment, Claire didn't recognize him. He had cut the auburn from the tips of his hair and gelled the short gray spikes that remained.

'You need to back up and get out of my way,' he said.

Slowly, she opened her door and got out of the car.

'Nice place,' she said. It really was OK for him. It was the way he wanted to live and be now. Still, he owed her information.

'I'm surprised you'd pull some cheesy little ploy like this, dropping by unannounced. But nothing you do can surprise me now, Claire. Just please don't make me have to change my phone number.'

'There's no need for that, Danny. All I need is a minute.'

'Which I don't have right now.' He glanced down at his toes, which looked like he'd had a pedicure. 'Client of ours is having a party.'

'Ours?'

'Mine, OK?'

'And you have a date?'

He sighed, picked up the large white ice chest he had put down next to the driveway and heaved it into the back of the truck. 'You think I can't find a woman to go out with me?'

'That's not what I meant. I came here because I need to ask you something, and I want an honest answer.'

'Seems to me like you came to judge.' He looked at her, especially her hair.

She felt herself flush.

'Just for the record,' he said, 'I'm not the only one who's changed my look.'

'So I'm wearing it down. Big deal.' Claire started to explain more and then realized that not only was he distracting her with the argument about her hairstyle, but that he knew exactly what he was doing.

'All I want is the truth about who called you about Al and me.'

He started to protest and she put up her hand.

'And don't say it was Al because I know it wasn't.'

'What if I say you're wrong?'

'You won't.' She moved closer to him.

'What makes you so sure?'

'Because you loved me too much once to lie to me right now.'

'Enough.' He turned and waved her away from him.

'Don't,' she said, and he stopped. 'You pulled me, maybe dragged me out of my shell, Danny.' She fought back tears but kept talking, keeping her voice firm. 'Without you, I would have been like my parents and my brother. I wouldn't have any idea how to stand here right now, to feel pain, admit it, and to ask you to tell me the truth.'

He leaned against his truck, and she could almost count the beads of sweat on his forehead.

'You did the worst thing to me a woman could ever do to a man.'

'That was never my intention. If you hadn't received that call, I would have tried to make it up to you. We could have kept going.'

'While you kept cheating?' He straightened the cooler in the truck bed and looked over at her.

'No,' she said. 'I felt guilty, I felt terrible, and I wanted to work it out. I didn't get a chance, though, and you convinced me without saying so directly that Al made that call.'

'I shouldn't have done that.' He leaned against the side of the truck and they faced each other. 'I couldn't believe you'd pick him over me.'

'And now?'

'I'm running late.' His voice had lost its edge. 'Maybe we can talk tomorrow.'

'I need to know now.'

'Because of him.' Danny yanked open the door on the driver's side. 'Because you still want him.'

'Because of me.' She almost reached out for him but knew she had to do it with her voice. 'There's more going on than I can explain to you right now, and whatever happened started with that call you got about Al.'

'Al and you.' One hand on the door, he stopped. 'I loved you, Claire.'

'I loved you, too. I still do.'

'OK.' He slammed the door shut and faced her. 'So maybe I did want to punish you. Would you blame me?'

It wasn't Al. It wasn't Al. The words rang through her head. Finally, she had the confirmation she needed.

'Thank you,' she said. 'Now, please tell me the rest of it.'

'The person who told me actually saw the two of you together.'

Only three people had remained behind downstairs in Al's office that night, drinking too much, taking their time leaving, walking out onto the mall and maybe even back inside. Tessa, Wally and Rosemary. A chill spread over Claire.

'Rosemary,' she whispered. 'Why didn't you tell me?'

'So you could be with Al?'

'I needed to know that.' She started to reach out to him but clasped her hands together. 'You must have heard that they found that rental car, that it was Rosemary's rental. But did you know that she listed your number as her backup? Danny, where is she?'

A plane buzzed overhead and she jumped. Then Claire realized it wasn't a jet, just one of Danny's new neighbors' planes, heading for its own hangar. He waited until the noise died away.

'If I tell you,' he said, 'it can't ever come back to me. I'm trying to start a new life.'

So was Claire, but he didn't care about that. 'Where is Rosemary?' she asked. 'In town?'

He was the one who flushed now. 'She's afraid. Terrified.'

'Because they found her rental car. How did it get in the river?'

'I can't tell you that. I don't have any idea.'

'And you're helping her because she was your source about Al and me?'

'Don't start slinging accusations, Claire. I've told you what I can.' He opened the truck door and climbed in this time. Before he could close it, Claire grabbed hold of the handle.

'Wait.'

'No. No more waiting. I've helped you enough.'

For the first time, Claire wondered if the destruction of her marriage began long before the night with Al.

'Where is she?' Claire demanded.

Danny turned on the ignition. 'The cabin.'

'Our cabin?' Her mind scrambled to make sense of the words. 'You let Rosemary stay in our cabin?'

'I owe her,' he said. 'Get back in your car and pull out, please. I don't want to crash into it and, thanks to you, I'm already late.'

Claire got to the cabin at around two o'clock. As she pulled into the narrow driveway, she flashed back on all those times she and Danny had sat on the back balcony before or after hiking the forest with Tessa and Eric. They had been her version of happy then. Now, as Claire stared at the A-frame with its loft, she wondered if she had been the only one lying to herself. And if Rosemary really were in here, it would be the ultimate betrayal by Danny, one Claire had never imagined him capable of. He would let Rosemary stay here in this cabin for only one reason, and that was payback for her telling him about Al and Claire.

It had never been an anonymous call, as Danny had claimed. The phone call that had destroyed her marriage had been Rosemary reporting to Claire's husband. If Danny had only told her that, they might have had a chance. No, that wasn't true. Had Danny told her, she and Al were the ones who might have had a chance. Even though Danny had left her, he made sure she would not be able to trust Al enough to continue what they had started.

She stepped out of the car, and the scent of pine was so strong that the memories almost crushed her. This had smelled like home once, like fun. Most of all, it reminded her of breaking out of her shell, of being someone other than her parents' daughter, of being spontaneous and having friends, not just colleagues. She had once believed that nothing here could go wrong. But something had. Claire forced herself to walk up the path and the two steps leading to the front door.

She knocked and said, 'I know you're in there, Rosemary.'

No answer.

'All right, then. I have a key and I'm coming inside.'

She twisted the knob, just to be sure it was locked. The handle didn't budge.

'Fine,' she said. 'I gave you a chance.'

Locks clicked and the door flew open. Rosemary stood just inside wearing jeans and a white sweater only slightly paler than her face.

'You need to leave.' In her right hand, she held one of Claire's kitchen knives.

'I knew Danny would warn you.' Claire kept her voice firm and forced herself to ignore the knife. 'He owes you that, I guess, after what you told him about Al and me.'

Rosemary's usually sleek hair fell in strands around her face. She looked at the knife and said, 'I mean it.'

'Guess you never tried to cut a steak with that,' Claire said. 'Asking me to leave is a bad idea, too. You and I need to talk more now than ever. I know that was your rental car in the river. So does the sheriff.'

Rosemary's arms collapsed to her sides and the knife hung there in her right hand.

'I didn't have anything to do with it.'

'But you did.' Claire knew she didn't dare step inside that cabin. 'Come outside,' she said.

'I'm not about to go anywhere with you.' Rosemary moved back, as if she could disappear inside.

'We have to talk about your rental car,' Claire said. 'If you won't tell me the truth, I'll have to let the sheriff's department know where you are.'

'You can't do that.' Rosemary stepped toward the door. 'I don't know how that car got out there.'

'You're going to have to do better than that.' Claire took her phone out of the pocket of her jacket.

'Wait.'

The door swung open. Rosemary stepped outside. 'Please don't call anyone.'

This woman had tried to destroy Claire's marriage. She realized that now. Rosemary could not even meet her gaze.

'Danny told me why he let you stay here.'

'All I did was tell him what I saw.' Rosemary cowered by the door, one hand on the knob.

'Why?' The thought and the memory had bothered Claire since that night, even before Danny had told her about his anonymous phone call. 'Everyone was walking out on the mall. What were you and Wally still doing downstairs anyway?'

'Nothing.'

'You were,' Claire said. 'You told Danny about me because you wanted to distract me, or him, from whatever was going on that night.'

Rosemary closed the door behind her. 'Let's walk,' she said.

'Not now.' Claire gestured toward the house, *her* house. 'What's inside there that you don't want me to see?'

'Nothing.' She grabbed hold of the post holding up the expanse of roof over the porch. 'No one.'

'So why don't you want me to go inside my own home?'

'Because.' Rosemary straightened. She pulled her hair back into something resembling the tight bun she usually wore. 'I have maps spread out in there, and I don't want you or anyone else looking at my travel plans.'

Claire leaned on the opposite post. 'What else are you afraid of? The sheriff has already traced the rental car to you.'

'I don't know anything about that.' She looked down and then back up at Claire.

'Because you ran the moment you saw it. You would have attacked me if you thought you could have. Tell me the rest of it. What happened to that car?'

'I'm not sure,' she said.

'Does it have anything to do with Wally?'

'Certainly not.' The huff returned to her voice. 'Wally had concerns of his own but he didn't know anything about the car.' She walked out toward the front of the drive, where the air blew in chilly and clean. 'I loaned it on to someone a couple of months ago.'

'And that someone had an accident?' Claire followed her down the drive. 'Only one person is missing. You loaned it to Natalia, didn't you? After she left Al. And that's how his gun got there.'

'That's not a crime.' Tears filled her eyes. 'She was supposed to drive to the airport in San Francisco and leave it there.'

'What was wrong with her own car?'

'She sold it once she vacated the condo and put her belongings in a storage locker.'

'Why?' Claire tried to visualize Natalia with her elegant clothes and her strong, proud beauty. She remembered the photo Al used to keep in his office of the two of them, him in a suit, Natalia in a fitted light-blue dress.

Only one explanation made sense. Natalia was the woman Tessa claimed to see on the river.

'It's her body we found,' Claire said. 'Isn't it?'

'Right now, I'm too scared to try to find out.' Rosemary sank down on a redwood bench outside the door.

'You have to tell me.' Claire sat down beside her. 'Why was Natalia in such a hurry to get out of here with no traces?'

'Al was following her, acting crazy. She was afraid he'd find out why she left him, and she couldn't risk that.'

Al had always said she married him only to get US citizenship, and Claire had never questioned that. They had been married so briefly that she'd never got to know Natalia well, and that had been fine with both of them.

'Why did she leave him?' Claire asked.

'Another man.' Rosemary's voice was stronger, more in control. 'He was supposed to meet her in San Francisco and fly to Austria with her to spend time with her family.'

'What about the car? Were you going to pick it up in San Francisco?'

'She was just going to turn it in,' Rosemary said. 'When she told me she needed it a few weeks longer, I was all right with it. They were in love. What could I say?'

The breeze across Claire's face felt like a freezing wind. Natalia had left Al for another man, a man who loved her, too. She could understand why Rosemary would agree to rent a car for her.

'When was the last time you heard from her?' Claire asked.

'An email about a week after the body was found but nothing since then.' She looked down at her clenched hands. 'Now, don't you see why I needed to hide? Don't blame Danny for helping me. He doesn't know anything.'

'Because all you did was sabotage my marriage,' Claire said. 'You were covering up something else, weren't you?'

'We were friends,' she said. 'Best friends. And she was in love with him.'

Again, Claire remembered those nights at Al's office after he and Natalia broke up. She recalled their social lives before their divorce, remembered Bobby Glover's charity fundraisers before the breakup, Natalia involved in conversation with Eric. No, not Eric. Claire couldn't even speak it.

Yet she knew. She knew. That explained why Natalia hated Tessa, and why Rosemary did too.

'If Natalia was in your car, she's dead,' she told her. 'All they need to do is match DNA.'

'I know.'

'They found the body weeks ago,' she said. 'Why do you suppose you were still getting messages from her?'

Rosemary looked down at her hands again, twisting the large sapphire on her finger.

'Answer me. He wanted you to think she was still alive so you wouldn't report her missing.' Claire took a breath. 'Eric.'

'Yes.' Rosemary shot to her feet. 'Eric. He's the only one who could be emailing.'

TWENTY-TWO

Tessa

Tessa keeps her jacket on that afternoon, even though the house is warm. She needs to hide the scratches. The girl is getting violent now. Tessa doesn't remember how she was attacked, but she knows the girl is the reason for the marks on her arm.

She sits on her bed, putting a puzzle together. Takes it apart, puts it together again. Takes it apart.

Her bedroom door opens and Jake comes in, wearing his new baseball uniform. He looks cute in it and she wants to hug him.

'What are you doing, Mom?' he asks.

'Playing with a puzzle.' She pats the bed. 'Want to help me?'

'I have to work on my science fair project.'

'Why are you dressed for baseball?'

'See you later, Mom.'

When he leaves the room, Tessa knows something is wrong. Jake isn't a little boy. He's in college.

She gets up and remembers where she is and why she is upset. She and Claire found a dead body and everything is going to change. She has scratches on her arm and she can't remember how they got there. Although she never thought she would have to spy on Eric, this is the only way now. Not a bad way, though. It's how she learned about that jerk – what's his name? – selling the golf place along the river. Winston. That's his name.

Eric's office at home is in a back bedroom that she never enters. She can listen from the guestroom but that's sometimes difficult. She can only pretend to clean it a few times a week. Tessa decides to visit her rose garden outside the room about the same time Eric says he has to make some calls. At least she will have an excuse for the scratches on

her arms. She won't have to keep hiding them from him.
She moves closer to the window.

'I'm worried, Bobby.'

The last person she wants him to talk to – Bobby Glover
– who treats her like a, what was that word? An appendage.
Tessa bends down and clips off a couple of dead roses with
her shears, not sure why she hates Bobby and his TV station,
only desperate to hear more. 'I know, but it's killing me. She's
harder and harder to reach. I'm not sure how much longer I
can keep her at home.'

At home.

It's all she can do to keep from crumbling here in the damp
earth. Eric breaks down. He is sobbing, and Tessa wants to
cry, too.

'I know,' he says in a broken voice. 'She's the only one I
really loved. If she can't make it through this, I don't know
how I can.'

More tears. She pictures Eric on television, choking up over
Gloria, his client, the woman who killed her husband in his
sleep. His voice sounds the same, and Tessa tries to bury her
feelings in the dusky scent of her roses.

'Right, and I've looked into that facility. I'm thinking maybe
just move into some kind of retirement community where she
can get the care she needs. They don't all have age requirements
and I'd do it for her. I'd do anything.'

Tessa backs out of the garden carefully, step by step. She
slips into the back door, over to the chair where her purse sits.
Forcing herself to breathe evenly in case he comes into the
room, she picks it up. Then she goes back outside, eases open
the gate, slowly so that it won't squeak, and runs. That's all
she can do. Run, without the car, without anything but her
purse slung over her shoulder. Once she knows she is safe and
that she is harder and harder to catch, she turns her phone
back on, erases Eric's text messages without reading them and
calls Timothy.

'I need your help,' she says in a clear, clipped voice.

'Where are you?' Timothy asks her.

'I'm not sure.' She looks around. 'Some kind of park by
our house.'

'By the river?'

'I think so.' She looks at the setting sun, the lights blinking up along the hill, the backyards, one of them hers. 'Yes,' she tells him. 'The river.'

In a few minutes, Timothy pulls up in the green pickup. She jumps inside before he can get out.

'Thank you.' Finally, her breathing settles down. Finally, she's safe.

'Have some water.' He hands her a bottle. 'I didn't drink out of it, honest. Just keep it in here for emergencies.'

Tessa gulps. The water is warm but she doesn't care.

She looks up at Timothy, who hasn't moved the truck. His eyes are large and he seems bolted to the seat. 'It's Eric,' she says. 'I heard him talking to his friend from the TV station. He thinks I'm losing my mind.'

'There's nothing wrong with your mind. I told you that before.'

'It's because I burned those pancakes. Because I got on that bus and because I saw that girl. The snakes. Everything else.'

'So you forgot the snakes at a school. Anyone could do that. That's nothing.'

'I think I forgot them the other day again.'

'So what if you did? And whatever fool laid out that counter area for the pancake breakfast didn't know what he was doing.' He pats her shoulder. 'And anyone can get on the wrong bus.'

The knot eases up and she can breathe. Finally, someone who isn't going to hurt her.

'He will never believe I really saw someone. I don't think Claire does either.'

'Probably wouldn't believe me either.' He widens his eyes as if saying more than just those words.

'Did you really see her, Timothy? On the river?'

'What difference does it make?'

'Because,' she said, 'I didn't need you to see that girl just to prove to Claire she was real.' The knot returns and she can barely get the words out. 'I needed you to see her for me to know she was.'

'Then I did.' Timothy reaches for the key and jerks the truck to life. 'I seen her just like I said, and I seen that guy with her, too.'

'Where are you taking me?' she asks.

'The one place you'll be safe. My sis. The beagle rescue.'

'I've got to let Claire know.' She reaches for her phone.

'Not a good idea.'

'I trust her.'

As he takes the narrow road that follows the river even father west, she thinks that maybe he didn't see the girl on the river. Maybe he lied to protect her.

'I hate to ask you this,' he says, 'but do you have any money on you?'

Then she remembers. 'I took all I had in the safe. Last night, I think.' She puts her hand to her lips. She must have been planning this, must have known somehow that she would need a backup plan.

'Good,' Timothy says. 'I can talk Ginger, my sis, into hiding you. She's good people.'

'I have credit cards, too.' She reaches into her purse and feels them fan out in her fingers. But maybe it's not three or four cards, it's one card she's feeling four times. Tessa doesn't know.

'That's all right.' He squeezes her arm. 'Hang onto them for now. You'll be OK with my sister, and Jack will be cool because of the money.'

As the road narrows and the river nudges closer, she's afraid again.

'If Eric finds me, he's going to have me put away,' she says.

'He'll never find you here.' Timothy slows the truck and she looks up to see the American flag painted on the side of a silver barn, sparkling in the remaining sunlight.

'The flag house.'

For the first time in more days and months than Tessa can remember, she feels safe.

'Why would you do this for me?' she asks him.

'You've been good to me. Besides, Wally asked me to.' He goes down the driveway and stops in front of the flag house. 'He told me, "Look out for Tessa. Eric is no good."'

She gasps and he tries to wave the words away.

'Wally said that?'

'He thought the world of you,' he says. 'Now, let's get you

settled. Believe it or not, even without heat, the place is pretty comfortable. You'll be fine, and maybe my sister will let me stay inside to look out for you once I give her some money.'

'What about Jack?'

'He's like those dogs of his.' Timothy laughs. 'Likes to think he's a bad ass but once you throw him a treat he forgets to snarl.'

'Take it all.' Tessa reaches into her purse and her fingers brush the gun. She takes it out.

'You don't need that now,' Timothy says. 'No one will hurt you out here.'

She zips it into the pocket of her jacket anyway and then digs into her purse again, finds her wallet and hands it to him. 'What did he mean Eric is no good?'

'It don't matter.'

'Tell me, Timothy.'

'Wally cared about you, is all. Said you was like a daughter to him.' He gets out of the truck, walks around, opens the door for her and helps her down. 'Come along,' he says.

Together, they walk up the path to the flag house.

'You've been here before?' she asks.

'Oh, yeah. Remember? I used to live here until Jack thought it was time for me to get my own place.'

'Right. I remember.' And she does. She even remembers Jack, who owns the gun store. Jack, who comes to pick up Timothy's paycheck sometimes.

He reaches for the door, opens it and they step inside.

The tiny space is covered with boxes. Along the walls, even on the bunkbed, rifles line up side by side. This place is like an overstocked gun store, including rifles that look like they could take out a lot of people.

'What?' Tessa demands. She can't believe he would lie to her but nothing else makes sense. 'What's going on, Timothy? Why did you bring me here?'

'Oh, my God.' He looks around at the collection of weapons, which she's certain are illegal. 'I don't know what he's done, didn't know he'd hide them here. Let's get out.'

He starts to turn, but a loud crack like gunfire sends Timothy to the ground.

Tessa screams as a man drops the baseball bat that downed Timothy, grabs her and drags her toward the beagle rescue van.

'I'm getting rid of this bitch!' he screams at Timothy's unconscious body. 'You're lucky you're family or you'd be dead, too.'

At the River
November

'You poor, dumb bitch.' Cool air washes into the car but Natalia's skin feels seared. She has expected anything but this, anything but Tessa's puerile name-calling. The woman must be truly crazy, more so than even Eric suspects.

'Maybe you didn't understand me. You can't possibly want someone who is staying with you out of pity.'

Natalia hates the way her voice breaks but Tessa doesn't seem to notice. She is grinning now, turning toward her in the seat, taking her purse out of her lap and placing it on the floorboard.

'You poor, dumb, delusional, narcissistic bitch.'

'Swearing at me isn't going to make it better,' Natalia tells Tessa.

'It already is far better than you can imagine,' Tessa says. 'Eric and I are together forever. You know that, don't you?'

'He feels responsible for you. That's all.'

'Responsible enough to have great sex with me this morning. Oh, of course. I just figured out the timing of all this.' Tessa sits up straighter. 'That's the real reason you did this tonight, isn't it? Because you're already guessing that he won't follow you back to Austria or wherever you come from the way he promised when this latest case of his is over.'

'We're going to get married.' Natalia forces herself to speak slowly.

'A little tricky, isn't it, since he's already married to me?'

'Not that tricky. Don't put him through anymore hell.'

'Oh, Eric might meet you for a time.' Tessa nods as if she has spoken in this patronizing tone before. 'Once, after one of these, he was gone eleven days.'

'One of these?'

'That's right. What makes you think he's going to leave me for you when he didn't for number six or seven or whatever the score is now? You're nothing but a symptom of an illness, but you're no threat to my marriage, Natalia.'

'I know better than that,' she says, and Tessa shakes her head.

'All I have to do is look at him and he's all over me. You're getting leftovers.'

It's her laughter that does it, her smug, sad smile. Eric had told Natalia about the other women. Bobby Glover's director of sales. Another attorney he had met on a case. A singer in Vegas. A psychologist expert witness for a client. One of his son's college professors. He had explained what had gone wrong in each relationship, how each woman tried to get too possessive and assume too much. Natalia doesn't care how many others there have been. She cares only that he said he wants her for the rest of his life. He wouldn't say that if it weren't true. What kind of man would just say that? What kind of wife would be so calmly acknowledging it?

'You're lying!' she says.

'You actually believed him, didn't you?' Tessa laughs again, her voice high-pitched and shrill. 'I thought you were smarter than that.'

Natalia's ears burn. Her throat tightens. She must stop that laughter, those lies.

'I'll be leaving now.' Tessa opens the car door. 'I wish I could stay longer but my husband worries when I'm out late. Besides, he's really into early morning sex, so I need to get back.' Still smiling, she starts to get out of the car.

Natalia lunges across the seat, her fingers around Tessa's throat.

Tessa struggles to push her away. 'Stop!' she screams. 'Eric, help!'

He's nowhere around, but hearing Tessa shout his name like that is too much.

She squeezes harder. Tessa groans, flails, grabs something out of her open purse and drives it into Natalia's shoulder. A nail file. Its stab barely grazes her. It drops to the floorboard, and Natalia remembers the gun.

As they struggle, Natalia scrambles for it and Tessa yanks her so hard that they both fall out of the car and onto the slippery bank. Then, still screaming, Tessa kicks and Natalia slides down to the bottom, to the river's edge. Lying on her stomach, her head pounding, she grabs onto some reeds and tries to pull herself onto her feet. A noise like an animal crashing through brush comes from the road. Natalia looks up the hill and sees the car rolling down toward her.

TWENTY-THREE

Claire

As the hours passed and Tessa still didn't respond to Claire's texts or phone calls, the gnawing worry grew within her. Finally, a text came in.

With Timothy and his sister. Don't tell anyone. All is well.

Claire locked the greenhouse and knew what she had to do. The phone rang for a long time, and she had almost given up when Al answered.

'You asked me to call if I needed anything,' she told him. 'I need something.'

'Where can I meet you?' he asked.

'I'll pick you up. Give me fifteen minutes.'

A text from Eric showed up on her phone. *T's missing. Need to talk.*

No. Not now. Claire ran the short distance from the greenhouse to the parking lot just as Eric pulled in.

'Wait.' He got out of his car and headed toward her.

'I can't,' she said.

Eric caught up to her, grabbed her by both shoulders and pressed her against the vehicle.

'Don't.' Panicked as she was, her calm voice surprised her. He paused but didn't loosen his hold on her.

'Not until you tell me where my wife is.'

'I don't know, Eric.'

'I'm guessing you do.' The wind blew his silver hair from his forehead, making him look older than he was or maybe only making him look his age. 'We're friends, Claire. Let's keep it that way. Just tell me where she is.'

Claire remembered the courtroom again, the way Eric could argue for anything he wanted, regardless of what was right or wrong.

'I know the truth.' She put her hands against his chest and

tried to push him away. 'I know, Eric. About your affair, your emails to Rosemary, pretending to be Natalia. You knew she was dead.'

His expression didn't change. Only his eyes. With peripheral vision, they scanned possible cars, possible witnesses and then homed in on her face, her throat. His fingers rested there.

'So you know. That doesn't change the fact that my wife may be in danger.'

Marching band members in uniform strolled through the parking lot, chatting and glancing over at them.

Claire glared into Eric's eyes. 'If you don't let go of me,' she said, 'I will scream.'

'I'm not trying to hurt you.' He removed his fingers and lowered his voice as if the band members could hear. 'Don't judge me. I love Tessa more than anything and I've already reported her missing.'

'Good,' Claire said. 'Now, leave me alone. I mean it.'

'Not until you tell me where she is.' In the fading light, his eyes looked so pale that the color seemed drained from them. 'I know you're trying to protect her, Claire, but as usual, you don't get it. You've got to trust me.'

'I can't.'

'You have to.'

For that one moment, his hands off her shoulders, his eyes pleading, Claire wanted to believe. She considered telling him where Tessa was hiding.

'I'm glad you reported her missing.'

'I'm not going away.' His tone turned conversational but his expression didn't change. 'I'll follow you.'

'Do that and I'll report you.' Claire opened her car door. 'I will report you to the sheriff's department, Eric, and I will tell them what I know. What you need to do right now is go home and wait to hear from Tessa.'

'If that's the way you want it.' The arrogance returned to his tone.

'It's the way it's going to be.'

'For now, maybe.'

He headed back to his car and Claire realized she was trembling. Afraid of him, she realized. She was afraid of Eric.

On the way to Al's office, she called the sheriff and told the deputy who answered everything she knew.

'Yes, that's correct,' she told him. 'Tessa said she was heading to the dog rescue on the west side of the river.'

Once she arrived at Al's office, she got out of the car and he came out of the front door to meet her.

'We've got to find Tessa,' she said. 'I've already called the sheriff.'

'Come on.' He grabbed her arm. 'I'll drive. You see if you can reach her phone.'

Al drove west, across the freeway and then headed north.

'Eric might be following us,' she said. 'He threatened to.'

'We can't worry about that. Besides, I don't see anyone.'

Al's jaw was set, his expression the way it was when he waited for the perfect photograph. These were his strengths. Patience. A keen eye.

Once they turned west again, the river road narrowed as they headed toward the flag house on the other side.

'Slow down,' Claire told him. 'I was there only once; I'm not sure where it is.'

Then she glanced to the right, toward the river, and saw a man struggling with a woman he was dragging behind him. A woman in a gray sweater and matching pants.

'Over there,' Claire told him. 'Oh my God. It's Jack, and he has Tessa.'

Al drove off the road and parked. 'You stay here.'

Claire got out of the other side but Al was ahead of her. He attacked Jack, who dropped Tessa in the struggle. Dazed, Jack swung and punched Al in the stomach. They struggled and fell on the riverbank.

Tessa screamed and headed toward the trees. Claire wanted to run to her but she couldn't. Jack slid into the deep mud surrounding the river, lifted his gun and fired at Al, who was just getting to his feet.

Al fell and Claire screamed. Sirens sounded from the distance. They couldn't get here in time, though. Jack, obviously dizzy, circled his gun in the air and then steadied it, trying to aim at Al once more. Claire lunged at him.

Jack grunted and staggered to regain his balance.

She hit him again, harder. Finally, he slid farther into the water. She fell too, gripping mud in her fists.

A shot exploded into the air. Tessa stood, holding a pistol with both hands. Jack collapsed and fell face-first into the river.

Tessa dropped the gun, turned and ran into the overgrown foliage on the bluffs. Claire wanted to follow but Al was wounded. The sheriff department's car arrived, slammed to a halt and two uniformed officers hurried to his side.

Claire pulled herself up and went in search of Tessa.

She traced her by her sobs. Crouched beneath a large tree, Tessa gazed up at her.

'She's down there,' Tessa said. 'Natalia. I left her.'

'It's all right, Tess.'

'I left her, and I just walked up the hill to my house.'

Claire stretched out her arms slowly, the way she would to a frightened animal. 'You're going to be fine.'

Tessa looked away. 'Don't tell Eric,' she said.

'I won't.' Tears filled Claire's eyes. 'I won't say anything to anybody. I promise.'

TWENTY-FOUR

Tessa

Tessa blinks back tears from her eyes and tries to remember where she is. Claire is crouched across from her so everything must be fine. The drone of a bullfrog comes from somewhere. Perhaps it is a mating call, perhaps a warning to other males considering invading his territory. Tessa pauses and waits. No one answers. Then there's a blurring of sunlight. Tessa squints and the girl's face comes into focus. When the light hits from a certain angle, this beautiful woman in the ice-blue dress looks just like her.

'That makes sense,' she says.

'What makes sense?' Claire asks.

'He always falls in love with them.'

'What are you talking about?'

'He always falls in love with them. That's all.'

Claire

The ER doctor told Al he was lucky. Al seemed to relax against the pillow and pushed his damp hair from his forehead. Squeezing Claire's hand, he looked up into her eyes.

'Yeah,' he said. 'I'm lucky, all right.'

'Those must be some painkillers you're on,' she told him.

'From now on . . .' His voice trailed off. 'I photograph only in color.'

She tried to make another joke about his drug consumption but she couldn't find words – not false ones and not true ones – for what she felt. Claire leaned over him and pressed her cheek against his.

His other arm came around her and he held her like that until the nurse came in, coughed politely and told Al he was being released. Claire could pick him up at the front entrance once they finished the paperwork.

As she rode the elevator to the lobby, Claire felt numb with both joy and sorrow. The words Tessa whispered to her beneath that tree kept returning to her and Claire finally understood what had happened. Still hearing Natalia's screams from the river below, Tessa must have returned up the hill to her home. The empty car then rolled downhill onto the tracks, where some time during the night it was hit by a train and thrown into the river.

But when Tessa walked into her house that night, bloody and disoriented, what had Eric done?

While she and Claire crouched in the mud by the river, Tessa had begged Claire not to tell Eric anything she had shared with her. As Claire hugged her and tried to comfort her, she guessed that Eric knew. This man she had once admired had protected Tessa. But he had also protected himself.

Although the hospital lobby was crowded, she spotted him at once. Wearing a jacket and jeans, he looked nothing like the high-profile attorney arguing his notorious case. He paced the length of the lobby and went through one of the glass doors to the patio. Claire followed. The area sat on an embankment overlooking the soft green of the hospital grounds at dusk. Eric stood at one of the steel tables, looking straight ahead.

As she approached, he spoke in a low voice. 'You will not say a word about this.'

Uncertain how he knew she had entered behind him, she walked up next to him and he turned slowly.

'Not a word, Claire.' His expression belonged to the courtroom Eric. 'I love this woman and I will not let you destroy her.'

Claire gripped the back of a patio chair. 'Which woman, Eric?'

Even in the dim light, she could see his cheeks redden. 'That's the real issue, isn't it? You're bitter because you screwed up your own marriage, because you don't have what Tess and I have.'

He glanced around the patio and she realized that this was

what he did wherever they were and whatever they were doing. Eric was always looking to see who was watching what he did and hearing what he said. But they were alone out here, and Claire could still remember how his fingers felt on her throat.

He wanted a showdown, a victory, and Claire needed to get to her car and pick up Al.

She turned and started back toward the patio door.

'Wait,' he said, but she shook her head. 'So you're that low. You're going to make her pay the price.'

'I think you've already done a fine job of that,' Claire told him.

That Saturday, Danny showed up on her doorstep. 'Our daughter's in the car,' he said. Claire felt her breath catch. 'She wants to invite you to her art show.'

Claire bit her lip to keep from crying. 'Thank you.'

'I should have done it sooner.' He sighed, and she realized this was his way of apologizing. She reached out and squeezed both of his hands. Then she released them and walked beside him toward the car.

'I'll wait out here,' he told her.

Liz wore white-rimmed cat-eye glasses that added a quirky vibe to her pale skin and blonde hair. As the two of them stood in the kitchen, she handed Claire a neatly folded paper bag.

'I brought a jacket you left at my place,' she said.

'I wondered where that was.' Claire put the bag on the counter and tried to figure out how she should continue. 'Thanks, Liz.'

'I'm going by Elizabeth now.'

Claire pressed her back against the counter. 'It's a beautiful name.'

'Dad's forgiven you, but I don't know if I can.'

'Forgiving is tough,' Claire said. 'It has been for me.'

Her lip trembled. 'I'm having an art show next month. I thought you could come.'

'Oh, that's wonderful, Liz,' she said. 'Elizabeth, I mean.'

TWENTY-FIVE

Claire

C laire remembered the moment like a snapshot, the late afternoon a cold black-and-white with just a touch of gold that lit the water. After working two weeks straight on the restoration project, she and Tessa had taken off and driven to San Francisco some three hours north. They took Highway 99 north to Manteca and then over the Bay Bridge, driving without music as they always did, no need for background noise. When they returned to the greenhouse with their prize, what little sun the day had held faded into the horizon. Even now, Claire felt the impact of that Monday like the slamming of brakes on a car. That afternoon, Tessa had forgotten Wally had died. That afternoon began a story that had led both of them to this moment, with Tessa in a prison from which she would never escape. Not a cell in the traditional sense, but a life sentence nevertheless.

As the bus from the adult daycare center drove in, she waited for Tessa, who was the first one off. Like the rest of the Green Thumbs, Tessa was dressed in a sage-colored logo shirt over jeans. The blue-knit cap she had worn the day of the San Francisco trip had been laundered so many times it had turned pale and seemed too small for her head. Yet Tessa's eyes came to life when she spotted Claire, and they hugged.

Claire touched her arm as the others headed for the potting table. 'It's going to be all right,' she said.

Tessa nodded, walked over and perched on the edge the wooden glider. 'I hope so.'

'I'll always be here for you. Do you understand?'

Tessa stared into her eyes for a moment.

'My friend?' she asked. 'The boy who tried to help me . . .'

'Timothy?'

'Is he dead?'

'Oh no. He's fine.' Claire pointed toward the river. 'Working today, but he'll come to see you soon, just like last time.'

'He's not hurt?'

'A lump on his head,' Claire told her. 'But he says it doesn't even slow him down.'

'Good. He's a good man. What about my son?'

Claire didn't want to say that Jake had been there every weekend, that he was moving back home and was enrolling in the university so he could be closer to Tessa.

'He'll be coming to see you as well,' she said. 'He'll be here all the time.'

'Did he win at the science fair?' she asked.

'Yes, he did,' Claire said. Then she told her the truth. 'Jake's going to be working part-time for us at the river conservancy while he goes to school. We can all be together.'

Tessa rocked in the glider for a moment, and then stopped. Her eyes looked empty and unfocused. 'Come back,' she told Claire.

'I could say the same to you.'

'It works both ways then, does it?'

'I don't know how it works, Tessa. I wish I did.'

Then Tessa glanced out at the river, as if looking for someone. She shivered and stepped out of the glider. 'I have to go,' she said, and went to join the others.

Tessa

There is a dot in the sky Tessa has been watching. No more girl, though. Just that tiny speck. She sits in the warm sun with her friends at the long table under the big tree, tapping the soft dirt in her pot, digging and digging.

The nice lady, her friend, starts to come over, but then her friend stops and looks over at the big car and the man getting out of it.

In that moment of sunlight pouring into the car, Tessa thinks she sees a woman in the passenger seat, a dark-eyed woman in a heavy coat so drab that it could have come from a silent movie. Then Tessa blinks and, as the woman blurs, Tessa recognizes the man. He is a lawyer she's seen on TV and the woman is his client.

That's right. The man is her husband – Tessa can't remember his name – closing the car door firmly behind him and walking up to her. She starts to hug him, but she has dirt on her hands and he won't like that on his white shirt. She lifts her lips and lets him kiss her. He smells like peppermint and lemons.

'Having fun?' he asks.

'Just planting.' He's very handsome, this husband.

'Did you miss me?'

'I just did.' Then she knows he said *miss*, not *kiss*. 'Yes, I missed you. Very much.'

He looks back at the car, then down at her and says, 'Gloria Sudbury was acquitted.'

The familiar words jumble together.

'That's nice,' she says.

He crouches down like a man proposing marriage, his face level with hers now. 'I saved her,' he says, and Tessa believes he is talking about the girl on the river.

'You saved her? Oh, that is wonderful.'

He puts his hand against her cheek and she smells lemon again. 'I want you to know that I love you very much,' he says. 'You are the only one I ever loved, even now.'

She puts her hand over his and feels his heavy gold ring. 'I love you too,' she says, and wishes she could remember his name.

After he leaves, she puts the bulbs into the dirt and sprinkles the water can over all of them. Next to her, over there by the tree, is a long stem with a pretty purple thing on it. A flower. She gets up off the bench, goes over and reaches out for it.

The tall lady with the long, dark hair walks up to her and Tessa wants to run.

'It's all right,' the nice lady says. 'That's a jewelflower. You can take it.'

'I can?' Tessa reaches over and picks it. The flower smells like pepper, but it is beautiful and purple like the lady's shirt. Tessa hands it to her. 'I want you to have it,' she says.

'Thank you.' The lady takes it. She has tears in her eyes.

'You're welcome,' Tessa says. 'You're welcome, Claire.'

Tessa looks up at the sky again. The dot is still there, bigger now.

The voices behind her sound like the rush of the river. Then the river grows silent.

She stares at the dot and watches as it widens into a hole as dark and deep as the night.